REDEMPTION

REDEMPTION

S. NELSON

To my amazing mother. Your strength, guidance, and wisdom have helped to shape the woman I've become. Thank you so much for being an incredible role model. You truly are the strongest woman I know and I aspire to be like you one day. I love you more than words can express!

ONE
LILA

LOST IN OVERWHELMING worry, I almost missed what he said. My hands nervously ran up and down my thighs in anticipation of what was sure to come. There was only one reason Mr. Hicks would call me into his office, and it was a reason I always dreaded.

"Lila? Did you hear me?" he asked as he uneasily locked eyes with me. He fidgeted in his seat, no doubt uncomfortable doing this part of his job.

"Yes, I heard you," I whispered. "But is there any way you could give me one more chance? Please?" As tears welled, I tried my hardest not to break down in front of him.

"I'm sorry, but I'm going to have to let you go. My hands are tied." Once the last syllable left his lips, he reached into his desk drawer and pulled out a white envelope. I knew it was the end of the discussion when he stood, rounded his desk, and came to stand right beside my chair. Exhaling a breath, I rose up on shaky legs and slowly walked toward the door.

"Lila, wait." I turned back with a brief look of hope. It was dashed immediately. "Here, please take this. I know it's not much, but hopefully it'll help until you find another job." He placed the envelope into my palm, giving me one more guilty look before he turned away and reoccupied his chair.

"Thank you." It was all I could say, even though I didn't mean it. I'd just been fired, and *thank you* was the last thing I should be uttering. But I knew it was only a matter of time. I had been employed as a waitress at The Corner for six months and already had to take time off unexpectedly. I was taking care of my sick mother, and she needed me more than I needed to wait on customers. Actually, that wasn't true. I needed to get those tips and the measly hourly pay to help with her medical bills.

Defeated and tired, I left the restaurant and walked toward my car, the parting gift from Mr. Hicks crinkling the tighter I held it. The weather was changing, the days becoming a little more brisk. Late September in Michigan was sometimes a bit chilly. The crispness of the air only added to my dread, indicating life was about to get drearier.

Once situated behind the wheel, I ripped open the envelope to see what was inside. I quickly scanned the check and realized it was the equivalent to a month's salary, and considering a waitress's pay was crap to begin with, it certainly wasn't much. How was that supposed to last me until I found another job? It was barely enough for a week's grocery bill, but I supposed he could've kicked me out with nothing but my wounded pride.

A muffled noise sounded inside my purse, startling me enough to forget my new reality for a moment. When I checked the screen, I saw it was my best friend Eve. We'd met years prior when we worked for the same catering company, and had been inseparable ever since.

"Hey, girly girl, what's up?" she sang, her voice as happy as could be. She was one of those people who were forever in a good mood. The only time I'd ever witnessed her cry was when her dog of fifteen years died. She was inconsolable for three days. Other than that, she always had a big smile on her face. She said life was too damn short to sweat the small shit.

I needed some of her positivity to rub off on me right then.

"Hey yourself," I squeaked, barely able to hide my depressed mood.

"Lila, what's wrong?"

"I got fired. Again. I don't know how much more of this I can take," I blurted. "Seriously." My chin wobbled as I tried to hold back the tears, but they came charging out anyway, and I blubbered into the phone. She gave me a moment to calm down before speaking.

"How about I take you out tonight? My treat. We can grab a bite to eat, or go to the movies. Whatever you want. What do you say?"

"I really appreciate it. I do. But I need to go home and figure some stuff out first. Maybe another time, though."

"All right. But only if you're sure."

"I'm sure," I responded, counting my blessings I had a friend like her in my corner. "But thanks for the offer."

"Anytime. Call me if you need me."

A tiny smile curved my lips. Eve had experienced her own share of heartaches throughout her life, but her unwavering positivity had pulled her through. Her only sibling, a brother, died in a car accident when she was younger, and her father died not long after. Her horrible excuse for a mother had blamed their deaths on her, which was only one of the hundreds of reasons why I never wanted to meet the awful woman. The stories my friend had told me made me cringe. It wasn't until Eve was older did she find out her mother had mental issues, but by then, the damage had already been done. In my opinion, at least.

I drove the long way home, dreading having to tell my mother the latest debacle. I knew she stressed about our finances, which was something I hated; I needed her to focus solely on her health.

I always tried my best, and I knew *she* knew it, but it didn't help when I was constantly failing.

Why can't I find that perfect job that would give us the financial security we needed, all the while allowing me ample time to care for her?

Did any such job even exist?

I soon pulled onto our street and parked my car near the house. We lived in a part of town that was a little less than desirable, but it was the best we could afford. Our landlord, Mr. Hawley, had given us a break on the rent after he learned of our situation, my mom having a terminal disease and all. I'd be forever grateful to the man.

Since it was a rare occasion for my mom to be able to fall into a deep sleep, I entered the house as quietly as possible, careful not to jangle my keys or make any startling sounds. But that day, for some reason, she wasn't asleep at all. In fact, she was sitting on the couch, curled up in the corner, reading a book. The sight was foreign to me, but I took it in and smiled. I'd much rather find her like this than flat on her back in bed, staring at the ceiling and crying when she thought I wasn't paying attention.

"Hi, sweetheart," she greeted, lowering her book onto her lap. "What are you doing home so early from work?" She knew the answer before I opened my mouth; I never left work early and I never called off, unless it was to take care of her.

I looked away from her compassionate gaze, because crying was the last thing either one of us needed right then. I couldn't afford the luxury of feeling sorry for myself or our situation; I had to buck up and get on with it. Walking toward her, I bent down and gave her a kiss on the cheek. I loved her so much. I didn't know what I was going to do without her someday. Shaking my head to get rid of such thoughts, I straightened back up and headed toward the small kitchen.

"Did you want something to drink, Mom?" I rifled around in

the fridge and grabbed the carton of orange juice.

"No, honey. I'm fine. Why don't you come over here and sit with me." She patted the couch cushion next to her. "Tell me what happened."

After fixing myself a quick drink, I sat down beside her and regaled the same old story. I was let go, but I would find something new before the week was out, which was quite a feat seeing as how it was already Wednesday.

"Don't worry, Mom. I'll take care of us."

Worry danced behind her eyes, even though she tried to mask her concern with a smile. She threw her arm around my shoulders, pulled me close, and kissed the top of my head. The simple gesture almost cracked my façade of strength, and before I became a blubbering mess, I placed a quick kiss on her sunken cheek before standing. Making my way down the short hallway, I heard her call out, "I love you, baby girl."

Why did this have to happen to us? Why did this have to happen to her? Lillian Stone certainly didn't deserve any of it. She was a loving and caring mother. Before my father took off, she was a devoted wife, although my father wasn't a man who deserved her attentions. He ran around on her, and even though I knew she knew about all his indiscretions, she chose to stay with him. The nights he came home drunk were the worst. As far as I knew, he never laid a finger on her, but the words that spewed from his awful mouth were enough to inflict the kind of pain he intended. He was always sorry the next day. My respect for him flew right out the window the very first time I heard the names he called her, blaming her for his shortcomings.

I was all of six years old the first time I realized my father was not a good man.

Two years ago, she was diagnosed with stage-four breast cancer. The very same day he took off, proving how much of a coward he really was. What kind of man leaves his dying wife and young daughter to fend for themselves?

My father, that's who.

Once inside my room, I quickly changed my clothes. I had to search for another job, and there was no time like the present. Pulling out my go-to pair of black dress pants, I paired them with a white sweater. My two-inch heels completed the look. I made sure to pin up any fallen pieces of my unruly red hair so I looked somewhat together. First impressions were everything.

Especially when desperation came knocking at the door.

"Where are you off to, honey?" My mom put her book down again, boring inquisitive holes straight through me.

"I have to try to find another job," I simply replied.

"Lila, you don't have to do that right now. You can take one day and rest before you continue to kill yourself. You're way too young to be this stressed out."

She was right; I *was* way too young to be so crazy with stress and worry. I was all of twenty-five years old, yet I felt like I was at least fifty. But what other choice did I have? I didn't want to remind her that without me working, her fate would undoubtedly approach faster. That without a steady income, we couldn't afford a roof over our heads, food on the table, or the medications she needed to live the barest of life. Her prescriptions alone were half of my income, but she needed them. Although, they weren't working as well as they had been, because her condition had worsened.

I had a mission to accomplish, and I had to put my best foot forward in order for both of us to survive our latest setback.

TWO
LILA

A FTER DRIVING AROUND for a half hour, I finally parked my car, opened the creaky door, and stepped out onto the sidewalk, finding myself smack-dab in the middle of a small shopping district. It wasn't anything fancy, but there were plenty of potential opportunities for employment.

At least, I hoped so.

The first place I entered was a children's boutique. Even though there was no outward *Help Wanted* sign, I decided to venture inside anyway. After a quick talk with the manager, he informed they weren't looking for any additional help. The next place I tried, a pizza shop, told me the same thing. And on and on it went. Every single place gave the same song and dance: "We're not hiring at this time."

Frustrated and exhausted, I walked into a small coffee shop, figuring it couldn't hurt to try one last time before heading home. Maybe I was being hopeful, or maybe I was a glutton for punishment. It turned out they weren't hiring either. But instead of walking out the front door, I decided to buy a muffin, take a seat at an empty table, and try to figure out my next move.

I was deep into my own depressive thoughts when a voice

startled me. I glanced upwards, and my green eyes fell onto a lovely woman. If I had to have guessed her age, I would've put her in her late sixties. Her short-styled gray hair was pulled into a loose bun, pieces falling around her face in the most delicate way. She was dressed in a simple black outfit, complete with comfortable-looking black shoes.

"I'm sorry, honey. I didn't mean to startle you," she said as she helped herself to the chair right next to me. "But I couldn't help overhear you were looking for a job. By the looks of it, you've been at it all day." She smiled, and some of the tension drained from me; she just had that way about her. It was foreign, yet comforting.

"You heard right. But no one is hiring." I sighed, the familiar sound of despair edging its way up my throat.

She shifted from side to side before landing her brown eyes back on me. "Well then, today is your lucky day." She extended her hand. "My name is Beverly, and I think I can help you out."

I grabbed onto her hand as if it was my lifeline. I had no idea who the woman was, but I was instantly intrigued. She obviously knew of a place that was hiring, and I would be a fool not to at least find out what the position was.

"Lila Stone," I replied, as I continued to grip her soft hand.

"Lila," she murmured, before a quick smile lifted the corners of her mouth. "What a beautiful name. But then again, it's fitting. Yup." She nodded. "Certainly fitting for such a stunning girl."

I quickly looked away, her compliment making me uneasy. I knew I wasn't unattractive, but the woman's eyes drank me in like she'd stumbled upon some sort of exotic creature.

"Thank you" was the only thing I could muster, my gaze fixated on the floor. After a moment, I lifted my head, a tight grin plastered on my face, knowing I needed to find out more about what she was proposing. "So, Beverly, how do you think you can help me?" There was no time like the present to find out whether my life was going to become easier or harder.

"Well, as luck would have it, I'm retiring from my job. And it's my duty to find my replacement." She took a slow sip from her coffee and continued to stare at me. She winked when she saw my eyes get big before narrowing again in confusion.

"What type of work do you do?" I asked, taking a tentative bite of my muffin.

"I'm a maid." It was a simple statement but one that dashed all my impending hope. I had never worked as a maid before, and once I made my revelation, I was sure she would leave and take her proposition with her.

"I've never done that kind of work before." I broke eye contact with her to glance down at my trembling hands. "So, I'm sure you'll need to find someone else, you know, more qualified."

She ignored my confession, instead asking me a question. "Who do you live with, Lila?"

I raised my eyes to meet hers, and when I didn't answer her right away, she lifted an eyebrow, patiently waiting for my response.

"My mom."

"And do you help your mom clean around the house?"

"Yes. In fact, I do all the cleaning." Before I could even think to filter my words, I spilled, "My mom is really sick and I help take care of her."

I didn't know why I'd chosen to reveal a private part of my life, but I had just the same. Maybe it was because I needed to talk to someone. Maybe it was because Beverly had chosen the same coffee shop I had, our worlds colliding for an unknown reason. Or maybe I was simply making up excuses, because it had been a long time since anyone had taken a true interest in me, other than my mom and Eve.

"I'm sorry to hear that, baby girl." I sucked in a rush of air at her choice of words; my mom was the only one who called me that. Instantly and without warning, my eyes glassed over, tears threatening to make an appearance any second if I didn't reel it in. Beverly pulled her chair closer, reached out, and grabbed my hand.

"I'm sorry," I said, still fighting back my emotions. "It's been a long day. I was fired from my job, no one is hiring, and then to top it off, you called me something only my mom calls me. Baby girl. It's all just too much." I rubbed at my eyes and smiled gently at her. "I'm sorry," I repeated.

"No need to apologize to me, honey. Sometimes life gets to be too much and we all need to take a breather." After several moments, she stood up, pulling me with her. "Grab the rest of your muffin, sweetheart. I'm going to introduce you to your new boss."

She didn't even give me a chance to protest before she practically dragged me out the front door.

IT TOOK US close to a half hour to get to our destination. Beverly insisted on driving, promising to drop me back off at my car once all the formalities were finished. She was convinced I already had the job, although, of course, I had my reservations. For one, I didn't have the necessary qualifications, something to which she said didn't matter. For another, how could she guarantee her boss would go along and hire me, based off her recommendation alone? Surely, he would want to do a background check and the whole nine yards. Only then he would discover I'd had six jobs in the past two years. To any potential employer, it simply didn't look good. I was trying my hardest to remain positive and calm, but after the day I'd had, it was nearly impossible.

"We're here," she announced, parking her car and opening her door. I followed quickly, the gravel of the driveway crunching under my shoes as I was hit with the oddest sensation I'd been here before. Only I hadn't.

The house was gargantuan. There were six huge, white pillars at the front entrance of the home. It was the grandest I had ever seen, and it did nothing but spur the onslaught of my nerves.

The grounds were almost as impressive as the residence, manicured lawns sprawling as far as the eye could see. I didn't want to be rude and intrude on someone else's property, but all I wanted to do was go and explore.

Lose myself in someone else's reality.

As the thought entered my mind, it was pushed out when I heard my name.

"Lila, sweetheart. This way," Beverly called, walking ahead of me toward the front door.

"Are you the only maid who works here?" I asked as we stepped into the foyer. I almost missed her response, as the interior of the massive place had my eyes roaming everywhere, unsure of where to look next. Everything was so exquisite.

She smiled, and simply said, "Yes." She walked me through most of the first level, pointing out all the décor. I'd counted eight rooms along the tour, and we were far from done.

"Do you clean all these rooms every day?" I inquired, more than a little overwhelmed.

She chuckled at my question. Obviously, I'd said something funny.

"No, you clean each room every few days. By the time you make your full rounds of the house, it's time to start all over again. Trust me, you'll be earning your money with this job, but I always found it rewarding."

I fiddled with the hem of my white sweater as I continued to take everything in. "Can I ask you why you're leaving?"

"I've worked for Mr. Maxwell for almost five years now and have loved every moment. But I'm not getting any younger and I want to enjoy whatever time I have left with my family." She reached into her purse and pulled out a picture of who I assumed was her husband and three grown children. Then she showed me a separate picture of four smaller kids, probably her grandchildren. Drinking in the images before me, I was suddenly overcome with a twinge of jealousy. It was only my mom and me. I had an aunt, my mom's sister, but I didn't get to see her as much as I would've liked.

After I handed her back her treasures, she proceeded to lead me toward the back of the house. "Oh!" I exclaimed as we walked into the kitchen. Much like when I'd first entered the house, my gaze flitted from fancy appliances to the handcrafted cabinetry to the exquisite marble countertops. I had only seen rooms like this in magazines. "Is there a cook?" I prayed she'd say yes, because I seriously doubted my abilities to handle all the required duties.

"Yes. Norma."

She patiently stood behind me, giving me an allotted amount of time to become familiar with my new surroundings. I tried not to smile, but I failed miserably. I really wanted to work here, and if Beverly had been employed for almost five years, then the boss had to be nice. Right?

"I'm nervous to meet Mr. Maxwell. How is he to work for?" We were headed back toward the front of the house when we came to a stop outside a set of large wooden doors. She turned around to face me, reaching out to squeeze my forearm when she answered.

"His bark is much worse than his bite."

What the hell kind of answer is that?

THREE
MASON

I WAS SMACK-DAB in the middle of the daily shit I had to deal with, when I heard voices outside my office door. I wasn't too alarmed, however, because one of the voices was Beverly's. I should be pissed off at her for trying to leave me, but the old woman knew my affections ran deep where she was concerned. But there was no way I could allow her to retire, not without a fight. I was going to have to come up with an enticing raise—although I already paid her more than I should—or maybe I'd offer some extra days off during the year.

Right when I closed my email, praying I wasn't called out on another job that evening, my door swung open. Sure enough, Beverly was standing in the doorway, a goofy look on her serene face. Once she took a step toward me, I saw she wasn't alone. A stranger was standing behind her, shielded partly by the oversized wooden door, and partly by Beverly. The only attribute I could make out was a mass of red hair.

By nature, I was an impatient man, but I had to admit I was intrigued, allowing a perfect stranger to loiter twenty feet from me without an introduction while I tried to dissect my curiosity.

"Mr. Maxwell, how are you this evening?" Beverly eyed me

with caution, and once she saw she had my full attention, she gave me a look laced with warning. For what, I wasn't sure, but my guess was I'd find out in the next few seconds.

"Busy," I replied more sternly than I intended, getting straight to the point. I tried to peer around her frame, but she moved, continuing to obstruct my view. I had a great rapport with the old woman, and normally we were very informal around each other. She did a great job taking care of my house, and I accommodated her when she needed something in addition to what I already provided, whether it be money or time off to be with her family. Plus, I could trust she wouldn't busy herself in my private life, questioning the late-night phone calls or my last-minute *business* trips.

Again, my eyes averted to the woman standing behind her, but I could still only make out a pile of red hair. She was shorter than Beverly, probably putting her around five feet, five inches tall. Almost a foot shorter than my own tall frame. The more time she spent in my presence—although I couldn't see what she looked like yet—the more uneasy I became. I didn't know how to explain the odd feeling, but I suddenly became both hopeful and aggravated. The air in the room changed, taking on an electrical charge. My breathing came in shorter spurts and my chest started to constrict. *I'm becoming anxious.* I wanted nothing more than to yell at Beverly to move out of the way so I could see her companion, but that would be rude. And I had no doubt she'd yell at me because of it. Like I said, we had an informal relationship.

"I hope we're not interrupting anything important," she said, before advancing a few more steps toward me.

"No. Actually, I was just finishing up for the evening." *If this woman doesn't move out of the way in the next two seconds, I'm going to physically do it for her.*

"Good. That's good." She sighed, busying herself by adjusting the collar of her blouse. *Is she nervous?* Beverly seemed to be lost in thought, cocking her head and looking at me but past me in a sense. And just before I interrupted her little daydream, she spoke up, making an announcement that immediately put me in a mood. Well, *more* of a mood. "I would like to introduce you to my replacement." As soon as the words left her lips, she took a step to the side to finally reveal the stranger she'd brought to my house. There was no time to rationalize anything. My body took over, betraying me and making me feel things I'd never felt before, all at the same fucking time.

My breath caught in my throat.

My eyes practically bugged out of their sockets.

My dick twitched in my pants.

My palms became damp.

My heart thumped against my chest.

She was the most beautiful woman I'd ever seen. While she wasn't your typical model-like beauty, she possessed a quiet, reserved magnificence. One full of innocence and potency.

Her hair was pinned up in various places, but tendrils broke free and framed her lovely face. And those eyes. Even seated behind my desk, I could see how hypnotic they were. They were calling to me, begging me to search her soul and put out the fire within. Despite her best effort to hide under ill-fitted clothes, too baggy for her petite frame, I could still make out her womanly curves.

Before I spoke, I was able to rein it all in and go right back to the image of a man unaffected. I'd done a great job for many years of portraying that mask to the world, a façade that was needed for survival.

"We've been over this, Beverly. You're not going anywhere. So stop messing around and tell me what you want already. I'll give it to you. No questions." The whole time I spoke, my eyes flitted between the old woman and the vixen standing in front of me. Every time I looked at the redhead, I saw Beverly smirk out of the corner of my eye, something that irritated me for some reason.

"I'm *not* messing around with you. I've been telling you I'm retiring at the end of the month, but you refuse to believe me. So, I went out and found my replacement." She turned toward the other woman, grabbed her hand, and pulled her forward until she was standing only a few feet from me. Good thing I was sitting down, otherwise they both would've been able to see the effect she had on me. "This is Lila Stone. Lila, this is Mason Maxwell, your new boss."

"It's a pleasure to meet you, Mr. Maxwell," she greeted, bouncing her gaze from my face to the floor and back again. Intimidation rolled off her in waves, which happened to tamp down my own barrage of emotions. When her eyes came to land on me once more, the corners of her lips turned up ever so slightly.

She fucking smiled at me and my world stopped. The sound of her voice was light and airy, yet there was a sexy undertone to her rasp.

I had to get her out of there before I did something I would forever regret.

"Lisa, I'm sure you're a nice girl, but this isn't the job for you."

"It's Lila," she corrected as she took a step back.

"What?"

"It's Lila, not Lisa," she said in a more timid voice.

I rolled my eyes before continuing. "Whatever your name is, it doesn't matter, because you won't be working here. So, I'm sorry Beverly wasted both our time. I'm sure you can see your way out."

I knew I was being a dick, but I didn't like the feelings she cast over me, so I had no other choice but to dismiss her. I also knew, without even looking, Beverly was throwing me some nasty death glares. *I'll deal with her once the other one is gone.*

"Lila, honey, can you please wait for me by the front door? I won't be but a minute," Beverly instructed before turning her full attention back on me.

"Sure" was her only response, before she left my office.

I tried not to watch her leave, but I failed miserably. I almost hopped out of my chair just so I could watch her disappear around the corner.

Once she was gone, Beverly let me have it.

"What is wrong with you?" she snapped, coming around my desk to crowd my personal space. "Why were you so rude to the poor girl? You know what? Don't answer, because you're going to have to get over it, mister. I *am* retiring, and Lila *is* my replacement. She's going to start tomorrow, and I'll show her the ropes. You *will* be nice to her and not give her any grief. Do you understand me?"

I stared at her in disbelief. The old broad had never talked to me in that manner before, and it took me a few seconds for her words to sink in. Our eyes were still connected when I finally acquiesced. There was no use arguing with her any longer. I knew deep down she'd been serious when she told me she was leaving me, but I didn't want to believe it. But her standing before me, hands on hips and anger dripping from every word, I knew our time together was ending. "Fine."

"*Fine* is good enough for me." She turned on her heel and left my office and toward the front door, where Lila was waiting for her.

This is not going to be good.

FOUR
LILA

"WELL, THAT WENT great," I huffed with obvious sarcasm as I made my way toward Beverly's car. There was no way I was going to work for that man; I didn't care how desperate I was to find a job. I'd hit the streets again the next day, all day if I had to.

"Like I said, honey, his bark is much worse than his bite. He's just sore I'm leaving. Give him time and, I promise, he'll come around." Once we buckled our seatbelts and were on our way back to town, she finished with, "Plus, I won't let him bother you until he's used to having you around."

Yeah, that's comforting.

Against my better judgment, I agreed to follow Beverly to Mr. Maxwell's house the following morning. For as much as I wanted to stand up for myself and find another position, experience told me it was nearly impossible.

We arrived at eight in the morning and I prayed he wasn't home. I had no idea what line of work took up his time, but I hoped he had an office to go to. Little did I know, all the hoping in the world wouldn't make it true.

Beverly told me to dress comfortably, so I wore the only pair of sneakers I owned, paired with skinny jeans and an old concert T-shirt. She gave me a once-over and smiled when I tried to ask her if there was something wrong. I wasn't sure what her look meant, but I didn't have time to dwell on it, mainly because my new boss chose that moment to come strolling into the massive sitting room, doing a great job of distracting me.

He was an extremely handsome man; too bad his personality was apparently an acquired taste. He wore loose-fitted jeans and a plain black T-shirt, his look ultra-comfy. When I glanced down, I noticed he was barefooted. It was obvious he was in no hurry to leave his house that morning.

He stopped short when he saw both of us, his eyes becoming more and more fixated on me as the minutes passed. I was fully dressed, but the way he stared at me made me feel naked. But I couldn't look away from him, even if I tried.

"Beverly," he greeted, a warning tone to his voice. When she looked in his direction, she smirked, instantly putting him on guard.

"Good morning, Mr. Maxwell. How are you this fine day?" Even I knew she was goading him. I wasn't privy to their conversation after I'd left his office the previous night, but whatever she'd said convinced him to give me a chance. I could only hope he wasn't going to take out his anger and frustration on me, constantly picking at everything I did.

He didn't answer her; instead, he made his way back out the same way he came in, but not before scowling in my direction.

What the hell did I do?

It was as good a time as any to learn some more information about my new employer. "What does Mr. Maxwell do for a living?" I asked as I continued to dust the shelves in front of me.

"He's involved in a few different businesses." She went right back to straightening up, as if her answer was satisfactory.

"Well, what type of businesses? And will he be here all day, or does he have an office he goes to?" My thoughts wandered back to the image that had just been in front of me. For as much as I didn't want to give that man a second thought, he was slowly starting to ingrain himself in my mind. There was no denying my attraction to him, but I knew better than to be inappropriate. He possessed a hard-edged demeanor, like a warning for others to keep their distance. His extreme good looks were in contradiction to his true character; at least I knew that much.

"It's best for you not to pry into his personal affairs, which includes his business interactions. Trust me when I tell you this, Lila. Your only focus needs to be cleaning this house. Nothing more." Her warning certainly caught my attention.

"Am I in trouble here, working for him?" All of a sudden, I had an uneasy feeling.

I think she realized what she had said, because she took a step closer and placed her hand on my shoulder. "No, sweetheart. I'm sorry if I made you worry. You're perfectly safe working here in this house. Just make sure to mind your business and the two of you will get along famously. Trust me."

The weird thing was, I did.

Beverly walked me through each and every part of her daily routine. Undoubtedly, I became a little overwhelmed by all her job duties, but I knew in time I'd be fine. We were halfway through our day when we finally decided to take a quick break.

Meandering toward the kitchen, I eyed all the paintings on the walls, not really paying attention to much else. That was, until I ran right into someone. I instantly backed up, my hand flying to my mouth in surprise.

My boss had appeared out of nowhere and stood right in front of me, dressed in nothing but a pair of low-slung track pants. His breathing was quick and uneven, like he had just finished working out. The look of surprise on his face faded quickly, the mask I'd seen earlier reappearing and settling into place.

"You need to watch where you're going, Lisa." He tried to be professional, but there was a certain gleam in his eye that shouted he was being anything but.

"It's Lila. Not Lisa. I'm not sure what's so hard about remembering my name." My last statement was more of a whisper. He was very intimidating, and I didn't want to upset him, but I couldn't completely hold my tongue either.

"Oh, yeah. Lila." He said my name as if it caused him some sort of discomfort. I didn't have enough time to delve into it, however, because as soon as my name left his lips, he took a step closer and started fingering my T-shirt.

I was too surprised to even react.

"What is this you're wearing?"

Disoriented from him being so close, I remained silent. Instead, my eyes focused on his sculpted, broad chest before becoming fascinated by the ink covering his left arm. For some reason, I never pictured him with tattoos, not that I pictured what he looked like under his clothes. Okay, that was a lie. The man was ridiculously attractive and thoughts of him unclothed had snuck into my head. And if that wasn't bad enough, a sheen of perspiration covered his skin, indicating he had definitely been working out. I was so wrapped up in my own head, mesmerized by his body, his question took extra time to permeate my brain.

He gripped my shirt tighter and drew me in, so close I had to put my hands on his chest to steady myself. Then the weirdest thing happened. My mind instantly filled with images of the two of us, and they certainly weren't innocent. I pictured his head between my legs, licking and sucking every bit of pleasure from me. Then I pictured him on top of me, thrusting himself inside, making me scream out his name until I climaxed. Lost to my imagination, I wasn't prepared when he retreated, throwing me off balance enough to stumble back a step. When I finally regained my bearings, a flush of heat spread over my cheeks as I dared to look at him.

What is happening to me?

"What?" I asked, truly forgetting his question from seconds before.

"I asked what you're wearing."

"Oh. Beverly told me to wear comfortable clothing, and this was all I had." I had taken a few steps backward, needing to put some physical distance between us. It did nothing to squelch the feelings building inside me when I continued to stare into his dark brown eyes. He looked at me as if he was trying to memorize every part of my face; I found it disturbing yet oddly comforting at the same time.

"Well, it isn't proper work attire for this job."

He perused my body. Slowly. When he reached my eyes again, he uttered, "I'll order something for you." Then he turned and walked away, disappearing around the nearest corner.

FIVE
MASON

FUCK! WHAT WAS *that?*

The last thing I expected was for her to run right into me, let alone touch me. I'd be lying if I said images of her didn't float through me from time to time since I met her the previous night, but I chalked it up to simply being horny. I hadn't fucked anyone in quite some time, and my body hounded me to find a release, and soon.

But standing so close to her made my chest tighten, my heart aching at the thought of pulling her to me so I could taste her lips. When she corrected me about her name, yet again, my cock had come to life, thoughts of her feistiness extending to the bedroom. I knew damn well what her name was, but I acted like I didn't, like I couldn't care less about her. I acted as if she was insignificant.

Too bad I couldn't convince myself of the same thing.

The woman did things to me I couldn't explain, and the more she was around me—in my home, for Christ's sake—the harder it was going to be for me to resist her. I knew she felt it, too. I could see it in her eyes, could feel it in the way she drank me in, but she put up a good fight to appear indifferent. Same as me.

I had to get her out of there as quickly as possible. And I was confident I had the perfect thing to do it.

It was a few days later when her new uniform arrived at the house. It was the first day Beverly had left Lila by herself, and it was proving to be the perfect opportunity to get rid of her once and for all.

Ascending the stairs, I found her busy vacuuming one of the bedrooms. Standing in the doorway, I watched her swivel her hips in tune with the machine's movements. My hand quickly flew to my pants, adjusting myself before she caught me staring at her. Although, that might've been another surefire way to get her to quit. But as much as I wanted her to watch me stroke myself to her image, I wasn't that much of an asshole.

When she finally turned around, she let out a little gasp, the shock of me suddenly appearing something she apparently didn't expect. She turned off the vacuum and stood there staring at me, shifting her feet until she finally decided to speak.

"Did you need something, Mr. Maxwell?" I loved the formality that fell from her lips.

"I wanted to give you this." Her eyes drifted from my face to my hand, her brows clenched together in confusion. "It's your new uniform."

"Oh," she said, before tentatively taking a few steps toward me. "Thank you."

"You can change in there." I remained motionless, other than a quick jerk of my chin toward the bathroom.

"Did you want me to do it now?" She lowered her eyes to the floor, waiting for me to respond, her quick inhalation drawing my attention to her chest. She was shy, but I knew there was an air of feistiness just waiting to come out at the right opportunity.

"Yes," I barked, sounding harsher than I planned. But maybe it was better if I came off as a complete dick. It'd certainly move things along much faster.

"Oh, okay." She looked uncertain as she grabbed the package out of my hand and walked into the bathroom, closing and locking the door behind her. I only had to wait mere seconds before I heard her reaction. But there was a few minutes' lag before she whipped the door open so fast I thought she was going to rip it off its hinges. She strode toward me in anger, fisting the uniform tightly in her tiny hand. "Do you honestly think I'll wear this?" *There she is.* Her eyes were on fire, and if she could've killed me with a glance, she surely would have. "There is no way I'm putting this on." She tossed the fabric at my feet before clenching her fists at her sides.

Bending down, I retrieved the uniform and threw it back at her. It landed directly on her shoulder. "If you don't wear it, *Lila,* then you'll be out of a job." I crossed my arms over my chest and glared at her. "The choice is yours."

I witnessed her inner struggle. I knew she wanted to throw it back in my face and yell at me. But I was sure there was another part of her that weighed the consequences of her refusal. Whatever war battled inside her beautiful head, there was no way she'd actually wear that scrap of material.

Was there?

Did she need the job *that* badly?

Before I could finish questioning her dedication to this job, she whipped around and ran into the bathroom.

Surely, she wasn't going to put it on.

Surely, she was going to tell me to go fuck myself.

Surely.

When the bathroom door swung back open, I actually had to take a step back. The *uniform* I had given her was more of a sexy maid's outfit, not a real uniform at all. The skirt barely covered her panties, and even though she still wore her bra, her breasts were on full display, causing my breath to catch in my throat. I had never in a million years thought she'd actually put the damn thing on, but seeing her standing in front of me, practically naked, I knew she was more than I bargained for.

But I couldn't let her know it, so I went right back into dick-mode. "What do you think?" I asked her, a self-satisfied, smug smile spreading across my face.

Her eyes became glassy, but her posture straightened. She was doing her best not to break down in front of me, and I had to admire her show of strength. Too bad it wouldn't do her any good.

"Why are you doing this? What do you get out of humiliating me?" Her hand found its way to her hip before she pursed her lips. She was a firecracker, and I was definitely going to be the one getting burned.

"I don't know what you're talking about. It's the required outfit, and if you don't like it, leave." My voice sounded deeper the more desperate I became to get her to quit. The scowl on her face looked like she was going to give me a run for my money, though.

Her desperation for the job was going to be my undoing, in all senses.

Without allowing her to say another word, I turned and stalked from the room, my hand on my dick the whole time. I needed a release, and I needed it right away. And if I hadn't've taken my leave right then, it was going to be either her mouth or her body, and there was no telling what would've happened.

I thought about her image in the sexy-ass outfit the entire time I stroked myself, calling out her name as I shot my satisfaction onto my stomach.

SIX
LILA

I CAN'T BELIEVE I actually put the offensive outfit on. But more than that, I can't believe he actually threatened to fire me if I didn't. Sensing I wasn't going to convince him otherwise, I had donned the new uniform and had done my best to keep my head held high. In reality, I didn't have much of a choice. I was lucky enough to have found the job, which was purely by chance of being in the right place at the right time. Although, when I looked down at myself, maybe it was the wrong place at the wrong time.

I delved back into my work, doing my job the quickest I could so I could strip the hideous uniform from my body. I spent the majority of my time cleaning all the bedrooms. They required my attention, but more so I was hiding from him. He was the last person I wanted to see.

When all the rooms in the upstairs section of the house were cleaned, I had no choice but to venture downstairs. I hoped he had left, but I knew he hadn't as soon as I descended the steps and heard him talking on the phone, and my hopes were quickly dashed.

There were mirrors scattered throughout his house, but I avoided them at all costs; I didn't need to be bombarded with my pitiful image around every corner. I kept my head down and finished what was required for the day.

When the end of my workday drew near, I sought him out to tell him I was all set to leave. I found him in his office, engrossed with something on his computer.

With a quick knock on his door, failing to wait for the approval to enter, I stepped inside and stood before him. His eyes instantly found me. I was doing nothing but standing still; however, his intense gaze made me feel dizzy, like I was floating above myself.

"What can I do for you?" he grumbled, never taking his eyes from me.

"I just wanted to tell you I'm leaving for the day." I didn't have anything else to say, so I remained stuck in place. Silent. When all I really wanted to do was scream at him for making me feel like nothing more than a piece of meat.

"That's fine. I'll inspect your work later on and let you know if there are any issues."

"You won't find anything wrong; I can assure you." I took pride in my jobs, no matter what they were, and I did them to the best of my abilities. I wasn't about to let him sit there and question my work ethic.

At the sound of my harsh tone, he stood from his chair and swallowed the short distance between us with a few long strides. Stopping a mere two feet from me, he tried his best to intimidate me. The look on his face was stern, as if I were nothing more than an annoyance he had to tolerate. Before I looked away from his intense gaze, I saw some other fleeting emotion dance across his face, although I couldn't quite nail down exactly what it had been.

"I'll be the judge of that, my dear," he mocked as he proceeded to circle me, like a hawk zoning in on its next meal. If I'd thought I was exposed before, it was nothing compared to what I felt like right in that moment.

You need this job, Lila. You need this job.

He was behind me, doing God knows what, when I found my voice again. "Do I have to wear this ridiculous outfit tomorrow?"

A pregnant pause ensued before he answered. "Why wouldn't you? It's your new uniform." He said the words, but I sensed the hesitant inflection of his tone. Almost like he'd never expected me to really put it on. Was he trying to get rid of me? If so, why?

"This isn't a real uniform and you know it. I bet you never made Beverly wear something as asinine as this." The words barreled out before my brain could filter them.

"I like the old woman, but that is not an image I want to see."

Is he chuckling?

When he circled back around, the tips of his shoes a few inches from my own, I lifted my head and looked him directly in the eyes. His beauty threw me off. How could such an enticing man have such a cold heart? I wouldn't go as far as to say he was evil, but him being a nice guy wasn't something I would attest to, either.

Tucking a fallen piece of hair behind my ear, I stood up even straighter and waited for him to dismiss me. He could take his eyeful of my displayed body, but it was all he was going to get.

Ever.

Without saying another word, he broke eye contact and walked back toward his massive desk. It wasn't until he was seated that he gave me the official dismissive hand wave.

What a jerk!

The whole ride home, the only thing I could focus on was how much I disliked my new boss. Beverly had told me his bark was worse than his bite, to which I had assumed he was a surly man. He was so much more. Yes, he seemed testy and moody, but I'd never expected he was the type of man who would humiliate another solely for his own personal amusement. Because that's exactly what he'd done to me.

There was no way I was going to tell my mom about my day;

I didn't want to stress her out any more than she already was. No, it was my problem to deal with. Due to the impending darkness, I had the perfect opportunity to change in the car before going inside.

As soon as I walked in, I sensed something was off. "Mom?" I scoured the small space to try to find her. When there was no answer, I shouted, "Mom, where are you?"

"I'm right here, honey," she whispered as she opened the bathroom door, moving slowly toward me. She looked pale, paler than normal. She grabbed the front of her robe and cinched it tightly, as if she were trying to ward off the cold, even though it was nice and toasty inside the house.

"Are you okay? You don't look so good." I circled my arm around her waist and helped her back out to the living room. Her disease ravaged her body, and no amount of denial was going to make it any less true. She had put up a good fight, but it looked like fate was well on its way to calling in the debt.

"I'm fine. Just had a bad reaction to some new meds. That's all." Once she was seated on the couch, she turned her full attention to me and smiled. "How was your first day alone at work? How's your boss been with you?"

I had to do everything in my power not to react. I couldn't break down or appear angry. Either response would have given me away, and I didn't want to worry her. I didn't even want to think about it myself, so, I just played it off like it was any other job. "Fine."

"Fine? Well, I guess it's better than horrible." She laughed and patted the cushion next to her. "Come sit next to me, baby girl. Tell your mom a story. Any story will do."

Ever since she'd gotten sick, we would do this thing where she would ask me to tell her a story. Mainly, they were stories of how I pictured my future. For some reason, those tales always made her feel better. I guess she wanted to know I still dreamed of the white picket fence, a husband to love, and children to spoil. She knew she wasn't going to be around forever, and she relaxed believing I still had hopes and dreams.

So, I went into a favorite story of mine about my wedding day and how beautiful all the flowers were, how glorious the ceremony was, and how regal, handsome, and elegant my husband was. The funny thing was, when I was talking about my future husband, Mason Maxwell's face suddenly appeared, an image that certainly put me on edge. Needless to say, it was a little more than disturbing, so I cut the story short and made her as comfortable as possible before retiring for the evening.

What I didn't reveal to my mom was all my stories were just that: stories. I didn't believe any of them. I knew what my life was going to be after she left me.

But I wouldn't spoil whatever time she had left on this earth with such talk.

SEVEN
MASON

A FEW HOURS after Lila had left for the evening, my cell phone rang, scattering all my wandering thoughts. Thoughts of bending her over my desk and fucking her from behind, hard and fast. *I still can't believe she wore the fucking outfit.* The image was going to be etched into my brain—something I wasn't entirely upset about.

"Yeah," I barked into the phone, annoyed whoever was calling me was interrupting a very vivid fantasy.

"We have a job for you," his gruff voice snarled. "I'll text you the address. And you better hurry for this one. Time is of the essence."

"Isn't it always?" *I was really hoping to relax tonight.* To say I was a little irritated was an understatement. But whenever I got the calls, I had no choice but to respond. That was the way it'd been for the past eight years, ever since that fateful day when I walked in on something I shouldn't have.

The job only took a few hours, and I was back home before the sun rose. Taking a hot shower to wash the blood from my body was a normal occurrence, yet it was something I never got used to.

Crawling into bed, I envisioned a life where I wasn't called out in the dead of night to "repair" someone. A life where there was someone to share my bed with, someone to eventually share myself with. But the closer I got to sleep, the more I realized my thoughts were nothing more than fantasy. I'd never entrust another to keep my secret; it was too dangerous. Still, the thought of a woman to accompany me through the rest of my life lightened me enough to fall into a deep slumber. Even if that image was of Lila, the same woman who was wreaking havoc on my very existence.

The next day, I did what I should have done in the first place: I had an actual uniform delivered for her. Clearly, my little stunt wasn't the way to get rid of her, so I had to come up with something a bit more outrageous. As I was having my morning coffee, it suddenly occurred to me exactly what it should be. I patiently waited for her to arrive. It was nine in the morning, giving me plenty of time to think about the perfect way to execute my plan, a plan that was sure to make her run for the hills.

Lila evoked things inside me that I found disturbing. She confused me, all while drawing my intrigue to the surface. But in order to protect us both, I had to make my proposal. But I wouldn't fire her. No, it had to be of her own doing; I couldn't have any guilt tied to it.

Beverly had informed me of the girl's situation. I knew she had a sick mother at home who she was taking care of, which was why my new plan was perfect.

"I have something for you," I said as I saw her pass by my office door. She stopped abruptly before turning back around to enter. She donned the outfit I'd given her yesterday, as instructed, and my cock instantly hardened. *I'm sure going to miss that scrap of material.*

"Is it a thong to go with my lovely uniform?" Her words dripped with disdain and it took everything in me to hold back a smile. *She sure is a feisty one.* I had to admire that about her.

I didn't respond, instead holding out another package and

giving her no other option but to take it from me. She snatched it out of my hand, her lovely green eyes searching my face for something, but I had no idea what. Was she looking for compassion? Pity? Whatever it was, she was going to be sorely disappointed.

Because in my life, I couldn't afford either one of those emotions.

After she had taken her leave, I busied myself with some investment portfolios I had to review, trying not to think about the woman who was under the same roof with me. I saw the way she had looked at me, as if she was conflicted with being attracted to me and wanting nothing more than to strike me, if given the prime opportunity. In such a short span of time, Lila Stone had disrupted my lonely existence. Funny thing was, I couldn't decide if I was upset or elated about it.

A few hours later, as I passed by the study, I saw her dusting some of the bookshelves. She smiled as she worked, and it was right then I realized I had never seen a more perfect woman in my life. Her waves of red hair were pulled back in a stylish ponytail, her face void of any makeup. The new uniform I'd provided was a pair of black yoga pants and a black crew-neck shirt. I knew it wasn't anything formal, but I didn't require such a thing. I really couldn't care less what the women who cleaned my house wore. The more comfortable they were, the better they would clean. Right?

I decided to leave her alone for the rest of the day, to let her dwell in contentment until I made my move.

IT WAS ALMOST six in the evening and I knew Lila was going to be leaving soon. I had to admit I was quickly getting used to her being around. Even though it'd only been three weeks since we first met, it felt like a lifetime.

I kept the conversations to a minimum, afraid the more I

engaged, the more she'd infiltrate my world. Distance was best. *But after tonight, it won't even matter anymore.*

I was finally going to make her quit. I was going to propose such a preposterous offer that I was guaranteed she'd walk her fine ass out my door, and my life, forever.

Searching her out, I found her in the kitchen talking to Norma, my cook. I stopped in the doorway, my eyes glued to her the entire time. She leaned over the counter and laughed at something Norma said, all while swaying her hips back and forth, unaware of what she was doing to me. My hand instantly went to my cock, trying to dispel it from getting any harder.

As I parted my lips to speak, Norma looked up and noticed me. Her eyes flicked from where my hand was, to Lila, then to an invisible spot on the floor. Before she turned away, I noticed the slight curve of her lips. In that quick moment, Norma lay witness to the lust I harbored for my newest employee, and I was sure it made the old broad giddy as shit.

"Lila, come to my office before you leave. I need to speak to you."

Startled, she jerked upright before spinning around to face me. Her eyes slowly raked over me before absently falling on my face. I didn't even think she realized she'd just blatantly checked me out. Thankfully, I'd had enough sense to take my hand away from my pants before I spoke.

"Okay," she said softly. I turned around to walk away, and that was when I saw Norma's shoulders rising and falling quickly.

"Did I miss something funny, Norma?" She'd struck a nerve. I didn't need a third party throwing their two cents in, even if it was nonverbal.

"No, Mr. Maxwell. Nothing to speak of."

"Well . . . good then." My gaze found Lila again and, sure enough, she was still checking me out. If we were alone, I would most certainly call her out on it, making her squirm where she stood. But I wasn't going to do it with an audience. I cleared my throat to snatch back her attention. "Don't keep me waiting."

Turning around quickly, I headed back toward my office.

Thankfully, she was right on my heels. My sexual frustration had put me in a sour mood, and I feared if she kept me waiting, I would have been more of an ass than intended.

"You wanted to talk to me?" she asked, standing in the entry-way of my office.

"Why don't you come in and sit down." I strode over to pour myself a drink. I was going to need it.

"If you don't mind, I'd rather stand." I could sense the tremor in her voice. She knew something was up.

"Whatever," I said dismissively. Once I had the tumbler between my fingers, I took a seat on the couch, leaning back and extending my arm on the back of my leather sofa.

I didn't speak right away. Instead, I took her all in. It was going to be one of the last times I'd lay eyes on the glorious woman, and I wanted to commit her image to memory. Even though she wore all black, she failed at camouflaging her body underneath. Her hair was pulled back and it only made her strong facial features pop, her cheekbones the envy of most women, I was sure. Her eyes were the most beautiful green I'd ever seen. And her porcelain skin begged for my touch.

When the tension in the room had mounted beyond uncomfortable, I chose to strike.

"What did you want to talk to me about?" Her eyes darted everywhere just so she didn't have to look at me. She was nervous, that much was obvious.

"As you know, Lila, this is a very large house and it requires a lot of upkeep."

"I know it does."

I gave her a look, warning her to let me finish. "And as such, I am going to need you to . . ." My words were cut off as I finished my drink. " . . . move in here while you're employed under my services. This is now a live-in maid position."

Boom.

There it was.

I had laid the sword at her feet; all she had to do was pick it up and make the final swipe.

Her body trembled, and I couldn't decide at first if it was from anger, shock, or hopelessness. Her bottom lip quivered, and I knew she was trying her hardest not to cry.

Turn away, Mason. Turn away from her.

"You have a week to make your decision. Until then . . . goodnight." As if I hadn't pulled the rug out from underneath her, I rose from the couch and walked out of the room, brushing her shoulder in the process. I refused to make eye contact with her for fear I would take it back.

No, I had to do it.

It was the only way.

EIGHT
LILA

TOSSING AND TURNING in my bed did nothing to break the hold of anguish on my heart. *This is now a live-in maid position.* I couldn't believe I was back at the same crossroad. I'd thought everything was looking up. I was lucky enough to have found another job so quickly, thanks to Beverly—bless her heart. The salary I was getting paid was enough to take care of all our expenses, including the ever-mounting medical bills, and then some. And I'd been able to put a little into savings for the first time ever.

But all of it was being ripped from my desperate hands.

First, the ridiculous maid's uniform, and now this? If he wanted me gone, why didn't he just fire me? Why did he have to torture me so?

Unfortunately, there wasn't anything left to think about. I had to quit, and I wasn't going to wait until the end of the week to do it.

Well, maybe I would.

I still needed the money, after all.

But once the week was up, I'd be done. There was no way I could swing living there, under the same roof with him, and still care for my mom the way she needed me to.

Hours later, I finally fell into a deep sleep, the dried tears on my pillow pushing me into the darkness.

The next day didn't prove any better. The mood I was in was certainly sour, and I was shit at hiding it from my mom. Dressed and ready for work, I made my way toward the kitchen to grab something quick to munch on before I headed out the door. I needed as much strength as possible to deal with my boss.

If it wasn't for the fact he was dead set on ruining my life, I could've seen us developing a nice rapport with one another over time. I would've never gotten involved with him, although being around him did strange things to me. Every time he was near, a chill would sprout through my body. My nipples would pebble and an ache would bloom between my thighs.

My mind was a different story. I tolerated his presence, because I obviously had to. He wasn't a particularly nice man—not to me, anyway. But he wasn't outright mean to me, either.

He was indifferent.

There were times when I thought I'd caught him staring at me, studying me, but as soon as he noticed I was looking, he'd break the connection, huffing before walking away.

"Did you want me to make you something to eat, honey?" my mom asked as she walked into the kitchen behind me. She looked pretty good; the new meds must've finally been working.

"No, that's okay. I'm going to grab a breakfast bar and head out."

"Are you sure, Lila? Because I think you need to eat more," she said, grabbing my arm. "You're starting to become skin and bones." Her worried look told me she was serious.

"Mom, I'm far from skin and bones." I smacked my butt for proof, making her laugh.

"Oh, I forgot to tell you. Your aunt, Ellie, is coming to visit. She should be here in two days. I told her she could stay here with us. Is that okay?" I didn't even know why she asked, I'd never refuse a visit with my aunt Ellie.

She was the fun aunt, traveling the world, engaging in countless, sporadic romantic affairs. She was a risk-taker for sure, and I envied that about her. I was always too worried about what was going to happen next to ever be exciting. And since my mom was sick, I was even less apt to being spontaneous. About anything.

"Of course it is. You know how much I love Aunt Ellie. I can't wait to spend some time with her."

"You just want to hear about all her escapades; I know the truth." She chuckled as she grabbed a plate from the cupboard.

"Yeah, there's that, too." We both laughed and it was a nice feeling. It was almost therapeutic to relieve some of the tension building inside me. But I knew as soon as I stepped foot into Mr. Maxwell's house, all my tension would build back up, strangling me with all the impossible decisions I had to make.

Damn him for ruining my brief moment of serenity.

The entire ride to work gave me a lot of time to think. He said he'd give me until the end of the week, which I was taking as Friday, for my decision. It was only Tuesday. That gave me three whole days, four if I counted today, to try to formulate some type of plan for what I was going to do for a job and money. I knew if I spoke to Mr. Hawley, our landlord, he'd work with us until I found something new, but I didn't want to take advantage of his generosity. His kindness had to be a last resort.

I was still no closer to a solution when I pulled up the long drive. Thinking it was better to put all those thoughts aside and focus on trying to get through another day, I made my way inside the house and immediately got to work.

I started with some dusting in the formal living room, which was located off to the left of the entrance. Once I finished in there, I made my way to the other rooms on the first floor, his office being the very last stop.

Not sure if he was even in there, I knocked and impatiently waited for a response. I had only cleaned his office once with him in it and he hadn't stayed very long. Ten minutes after starting, he mumbled something under his breath about distractions and took off.

Mr. Maxwell was so moody whenever he was around me. I saw the way he'd interacted with Norma, acting like a completely different person. He'd smile, even going so far as to laugh at what she said. He engaged her in friendly banter and would express his concerns about issues they'd discussed previously, always asking if there was anything he could do for her. He was even that way with Beverly, the few interactions I'd witnessed between them before she left.

"Come in," he shouted. *Oh, yeah, I did just knock on his door.* I hoped history repeated itself and he took off soon after I started cleaning.

"I finished all the other rooms and wanted to clean this one before I went upstairs." Stepping inside, I set my sights on the large bookcase lining the entire left wall. When I dared to glance over my shoulder, I noticed him looking at me. He didn't know I was watching him at first, his eyes too busy capturing every small movement I made. The way he watched me hit me like a sledge-hammer, right between my legs.

His tongue peeked out and licked his bottom lip before biting down on it.

Ignore him.

When his intense stare made its way back up to my face, he stopped dead, knowing he'd been caught. Quickly clearing his throat, he turned his head so fast I thought he was going to snap it.

I chuckled to myself. *Good. I'm glad I make him feel uncomfort-able.* Because I sure didn't like my body's reaction to him.

After several minutes, he got up, and at first, I thought he was going to leave the room like he had the last time. I relaxed some until I realized how close he was, standing directly behind me. His warm breath on my neck made me shudder, and not necessarily in a bad way.

My arm was stretched above my head, dusting one of the bookshelves, when I instantly seized up. I didn't want to move for fear that . . . what? That he would move away? That he would do something?

I wasn't sure, and it was that uncertainty that slowly drove me insane.

Before I could formulate something to say, I felt his arm brush against my shoulder as he reached up and grabbed a book.

"Sorry," he whispered into my ear, all while leaning in closer.

What is he doing?

Deciding the best course of action was to pretend like nothing had happened, I ignored him and continued dusting, although at a much slower pace.

My mind was rattled.

I heard the creak of his leather chair as he sat back down. Any hope I had of being left alone vanished, knowing I'd be stuck in this space with him for the next thirty minutes, his spacious office requiring at least that much of my time.

When I finished dusting his shelves, still somewhat distracted by his presence, I walked toward him. I needed to empty his garbage can, but he was in the way. Standing by the edge of his desk, I glanced down at him, silent because my brain was firing off all sorts of demands, none of which would sound very nice if they left my lips. Seconds passed, and still he didn't acknowledge me, so I stole that time to briefly lose myself to my own thoughts. Wicked thoughts. What his breath would feel like on my naked skin, warming me to the highest degree of fever. My inner muscles clenched in anticipation and my chest expanded, as if my thoughts had become reality. I absently closed my eyes and tilted my head back, licking my lips in the process.

"Did you need something?" his voice rang out, startling me and dashing my short-lived fantasy.

Oh my God! What is wrong with me? Seriously?

"I need to get under your desk," I mumbled, not realizing what I'd said.

But he knew, because his lips curved upward. It figured the first time he'd smile at me was because of a misunderstanding, one he made inappropriate. Or was that my doing? Nevertheless, his smirk was sexy as hell.

"Oh, do you? And what are you going to do under there, pray tell?" He linked his hands behind his head and relaxed in my obvious discomfort.

All of a sudden, I missed my moody boss.

My instincts told me to keep quiet, to not engage him, but in the end, I told my inner voice to beat it. Then three words I never thought I'd say to him left my mouth.

"Don't you wish?"

And just like that, the air suddenly filled with tension, of what kind, I was still trying to determine.

"Well—" he started, but I cut him off before he could finish. I didn't want things to get any more awkward.

"I need to empty your trash, so if you don't mind, I need to reach under your desk. For the garbage," I said, a blush creeping over my cheeks the longer I continued to ramble.

I moved to stand beside his chair, but he didn't budge. As I reached down, he still made no attempt to back up. So I locked eyes with him, all while silently screaming at him to stop making me uncomfortable. As my lips parted, he finally inched his chair back from the edge of his desk, but not enough for me to do what

I needed to without crowding him.

"Well, go ahead if you're going to grab it. I have work to get back to." An air of cockiness drifted all around him, and I wanted nothing more than to run from the room. But I had to do this if I had any hope of escaping his office in the next few minutes.

So I moved in closer, leaning forward as best I could, and reached under his desk. The pail was only inches outside my grasp, so I leaned in farther, one hand gripping the corner of his desk to steady myself. As I was pulling the trash can out, thankful our odd and uncomfortable interaction would be over soon, I lost my balance and fell backward.

Right on top of his lap.

Oh. My. God!

I would surely die a thousand deaths. Disbelief shrouded my good sense and mortification took over. Not only did I fall directly onto his lap, but my back rested against his broad chest. His scent did nothing to calm me, instead weaving its sweet yet masculine smell into every lustful cell of my body.

He had to have been as surprised as I was, although he didn't show it. I felt his chest vibrate against my back. The sound of his laughter spurred my embarrassment even more. His hands gripped the sides of my waist as he tried to steady me.

Then I felt something hard press against my ass.

It was him.

He hardened beneath me, and I all but jumped across his desk. I took off out of his office so fast I was surprised his door didn't slam shut behind me from the wind I created with my fleeing body.

NINE
MASON

WHAT THE HELL *is wrong with me?* I'm supposed to be keeping my distance from her, not goading her and throwing out sexual innuendos. But I couldn't seem to help myself. Initially, I was going to leave her alone in my office, like I had the last time, but when I stood behind her, something had just clicked.

The overwhelming need to be close to her took over, and before I realized what I was doing, I was brushing up against her as I retrieved a book I most certainly didn't need. Thankfully, what she didn't see was me smelling her like some kind of psycho.

Then the shit I pulled with the trash can was way out of bounds. But again, I couldn't help myself. The whole time she stood beside me, her spunk trying not to get the best of her, all I kept picturing was bending her over and taking her hard. Making her whimper in excitement was the only goal playing over and over in my fucked-up head.

What I should've done was go find her to apologize, but my stubbornness kept me glued to my chair. Besides, I hardly ever admitted I was wrong—a trait I'd been told was rather irritating.

I was alone with my thoughts for the next hour, when my

stomach dictated my next move, and as I rounded the corner into the kitchen, I practically collided with Lila.

Why do we keep smacking into one another?

She was munching on some grapes, and the surprise of our bodies smashing together was enough for her to choke on one of those damn things. When she started coughing, I jumped right into action. My hand came down in rapid successions, pounding on her back until I deemed she was free from danger.

"Damn, Mr. Maxwell. What are you trying to do? Kill me?" she asked, backing up a few steps.

I wasn't sure if she meant because I was the cause of her choking fit or because I was pounding away on her delicate flesh. Either way, there was no mistaking her embarrassment.

If given the leeway, I was sure Lila would tell me exactly what she thought of me, but I knew she held back because I was her employer. Speaking of which, she had three more days to give me her decision. I knew she was going to quit, and I knew I was a real shit for making her do it, but I couldn't fire her. I knew it was the same difference, but still.

"I thought you were upstairs cleaning. Had I known you were down here, wasting time, I would have tiptoed around my own damn house." I didn't mean for my response to be so harsh, but I couldn't help it. I couldn't stand the way she made me feel, constantly wanting to be near her, to touch her, and be within enough distance to inhale her sweet scent. I was lashing out at her and it wasn't fair. It wasn't her fault, but I did it just the same.

Her light green eyes bored into my flesh as if she was ready to strike. But she didn't, biting her tongue instead. *I bet she'll let loose on me on Friday, when she tells me to go to hell for putting her in this predicament.*

I welcomed the fire, which was surely going to torch my soul.

"I was hungry, so I ran down here to grab something. I do get a break, don't I?" she mumbled.

Deciding not to answer, I moved away from her, opened the fridge, and looked around. Hoping she'd disappear back upstairs, I lingered for a little while longer. All of a sudden, my appetite was gone, much like my patience for the whole dance between her and me.

We both felt something, but there was no way I could act on it. I couldn't bring her into my world, and although I was doing a bastardly thing by basically getting rid of her, it was the kinder thing to do.

When enough time had passed, I closed the door and turned around, immediately sucking in a breath when I saw her standing in the entryway of the kitchen. She hadn't moved. Not a muscle. To make matters worse, she was checking me out. Her sultry eyes slowly drank me in, moving their way up my body, so distracted with her perusal she had no idea I was staring straight back at her, a small smirk dancing on my lips.

She's not as upset with me as she plays to be.

"Like what you see, sweetheart?" I couldn't help it.

"Wh-what?" she stuttered. "Uhhh . . . I was just finishing my snack." Her eyes grew dark. "I wasn't checking you out."

"Uh-huh," I muttered, before brushing past her on my way out.

Fuck! Now I need a drink.

THAT WOMAN HAD infiltrated my world with guns blazing. She wasn't obvious about it, though. She was quiet and reserved, except when I pissed her off, which was apparently quite often. I tried to feign indifference, but she saw straight through me. I wasn't fooling anyone with the, *I couldn't give a shit* attitude, especially not after the little stunt I'd pulled in my office a couple days before. I may as well have hung a sign around my neck saying, *come and get it.*

Deciding to man up and deal with whatever emotions ran rampant inside me, I vowed to let her go.

Completely.

She'd give me her decision tomorrow and my life would return to my unfortunate version of normal. Leaning back in my chair, lost in thought, I nearly jumped out of my skin when I heard her voice.

"Mr. Maxwell, is it all right if I head out a little early? My aunt is coming to visit, and I want to spend as much time with her as I can before she leaves again." There was a sadness to her voice, but I'd heard it loud and clear. For once, I decided not to be a prick and give her a hard time.

"Sure, go ahead." I'd almost said her name but decided against it at the last second. I had to start ridding myself of every trace of her, and starting with her name was the most obvious choice. I never looked up from my desk, and not until I heard the front door click shut did I breathe a sigh of relief. Or was it frustration?

TEN
LILA

T HE TIME WAS edging closer to midnight as we sat around
the kitchen table. Aunt Ellie had arrived a few hours before,
bags in hand and a look on her face I hadn't seen before.
Sadness.

Her hair was pulled into a messy bun and her face was void
of makeup—although she was a natural beauty, so it didn't matter
much. While she and my mother looked very similar, there were
massive differences between the two. My mother was shorter, only
an inch taller than my five-foot-five frame, and her hair was as red
and curly as mine. My aunt was taller, at five foot nine. Her hair was
a beautiful shade of blonde and it was poker-straight, something I
had sometimes envied. The one feature they shared, we all shared,
was our eyes. The light green shade of our irises was a beautiful
contrast against both our hair colors.

"So," she continued, telling us about her latest escapade, "Raul
and I were happy, living life to the fullest in Morocco, when he . . ."
She darted her eyes everywhere except at us.

"He what?" I blurted. I couldn't help it. I became angry, waiting
for her to drop some kind of bomb. I loved my aunt so much, and if
someone had hurt her, I wanted to know about it. I knew in reality

I couldn't do anything, but I wanted to hurt them just the same.

"Raul was so kind and loving in the beginning. I simply didn't see it coming." My mom and I both reached across the table at the same time, each of us grabbing one of her hands and squeezing, offering her our undying support with the simple gesture. "After six months of being together, he changed. He began questioning everything. Where I was going, who I was with. And no matter what I told him, which was always the truth, he never believed me. We started to fight constantly, and then one night . . . one night, he got so drunk he lashed out and struck me."

I gasped in shock. It hurt me to know someone had assaulted her. Then an unrelenting barrage of questions barreled through me. Who was this guy? Did he know she was with us? Did he do it more than once?

"I wanted to leave him sooner," she continued. "But he's a very wealthy man and he made it difficult for me to get away, restricting the amount of money I had at any given time. So, I acted as if I forgave him and continued on with the charade until I found my opportunity. He got called away overnight on a business trip, and as soon as I confirmed he had landed, I took the small stack of cash I had been hoarding and caught the first flight here." Fresh tears fell and hit the tabletop. My heart broke for her.

My mother moved her chair closer as her sister continued to cry. "Everything will be all right, Ellie. You're here now. You're safe and I won't let anything happen to you."

"*We* won't let anything happen to you," I corrected immediately.

Both women looked at me and smiled, even if it was forced.

"Well, you can stay with us as long as you want. Seriously, you don't have to go anywhere if you don't want to," my mother offered.

"I think I'm actually going to take you up on that, sis," she replied, moving in to give her a hug. "Plus, I'd like to be here, you know, to help take care of you."

"Now, you know I don't need you to do that. I'm fine. Actually, I'm feeling better these past few days. So don't go worrying about me." She turned in my direction and pointed her finger at me. "Either one of you."

"Mom, I'm always going to worry about you, no matter what. So don't try pulling the tough act on me." I smiled, lessening the tone of my words.

"So, Aunt Ellie, how long do you think you'll be here with us? Hopefully a long while this time. I've really missed you." I rose and walked toward the kitchen. I needed a glass of water; we'd been talking so much my throat had become dry.

"Well, now that you ask, I was thinking at least a few months. I could look for work in a day or so to help out. I'm still a registered nurse, so hopefully one of the hospitals is hiring. Eventually, I could get my own place, but for now, I really need to be with family." She turned back toward my mother. "Are you sure this is okay, Lillian?"

"Yes, of course. I'm thrilled you'll be sticking around for longer than a week this time." The love they shared for one another shone through their eyes, their undying support for the other a wonderful trait.

"Good," I cut in. "Now that everything is settled, I'm heading off to bed. I'm exhausted, although I've had the best night in a long time." I rounded the table and kissed Aunt Ellie before turning and kissing my mom goodnight. "I love you both," I called out as I disappeared down the hallway.

As I lay there, staring into the dark, a thought suddenly came rushing over me. A peace I'd been longing for appeared and made me smile.

I WAS EARLY to work the next day and surprisingly excited. A weight had been lifted the previous night, and nothing could steal the spring from my step.

It was Friday. The day I was supposed to give my decision. At least I wouldn't have to worry about looking for another job, or how we were going to pay the bills, or about my mother being looked after.

I was telling him I was moving in.

I immediately went in search to find him as soon as I walked through the front door. Checking his office first, a place he seemed to be in the morning, I was disappointed to find the space empty. I proceeded to make my rounds throughout the bottom level, but I still couldn't locate him.

Ascending the stairwell, I was lost in thought over the impending changes. While I was thrilled to still have a good-paying job, I was going to miss my mom and my aunt terribly. Would he allow me to leave for a few hours after I was done with my duties? What time did I have to be back here? Did I have a curfew? Was I able to come and go as I pleased? I had so many questions that needed to be answered. *And if I could find my freaking boss, I might just get some.*

I had checked every open room but one on the second level, and still nothing. There was one door that was locked. It was always locked. When Beverly first showed me around, she told me to never go in there; it was his private room and I'd be wise to simply walk on past. I asked her what was in there and she simply gave me a look, one that told me to mind my own business. Of course, I was even more curious than ever after that, but I'd follow her rules.

His rules, essentially.

Finally, I came upon the last door on the right: his bedroom. I had only gone in there to clean, but knowing he was probably in there suddenly made me nervous. Anxious. A light perspiration broke out on my forehead, and when I raised my arm up to wipe it away, I noticed my hand shaking. My breathing had accelerated while my heart hammered violently against my chest.

Lightly knocking on the door, I stood still while trying to calm down. When there was no answer, I knocked harder. Still nothing. *Maybe he's not even in there.* The longer the door remained closed, the more my nerves subsided.

Deciding to enter, I turned the handle and stepped inside. My eyes instantly searched the room. "Mr. Maxwell. Are you in here?" I called out as I moved farther and farther into his bedroom. "Mr. Maxwell?"

Suddenly, I heard a noise coming from the bathroom. Before I could retreat, however, the door swung open and my boss entered his bedroom in nothing but a towel, the steam from his shower swirling behind him. When our eyes locked, I knew it was too late for me to escape. I didn't know what else to do, so as I stood there motionless, all my words failing to come to life, I took in the sight before me. Shamelessly.

Water cascaded down his sculpted chest and disappeared beneath the white fabric concealing his manhood. He raised his arms to run his hands through his wet hair, the ink covering his arm coming to life with the subtle movement.

He was perfection.

He was my boss.

We were going to be living under the same roof.

I tried not to think about all that as I lived out some sort of fantasy in my head. It never failed; whenever we were in close proximity of each other, my brain filled with naughty thoughts of the man.

I envisioned him dropping his towel as he stalked toward me, reaching out to draw me closer, soaking my clothes with his still-wet body. His lips would descend and devour me, teasing me until my panties were soaked with desire. I'd drop to my knees when he finally released me and take him into my mouth, pleasing him until he roared out his release.

"Lila," he interrupted, tearing me from my drifting thoughts. "What are you doing in here?" He didn't sound upset, but he was clearly confused. His dark eyes fixated on me, making me squirm the more we stood there. Him practically naked.

Did I mention he was only wearing a towel?

"Oh . . . s-sorry," I stammered. "I needed to talk to you and couldn't find you." I finally turned around and broke the uneasy tension building between us. "I'll wait for you in your office." I rushed out of there so fast you would have thought the room was on fire. I swore I heard him laughing as I ran down the hallway.

ELEVEN
MASON

WHY, JUST WHEN I thought I was going to be successful in ridding any thoughts of that woman, does she appear in front of me and refuel all my desires?

I'd never wanted to throw caution to the wind so much before and say fuck it. I wanted to rush her and throw her down on my bed. The way she watched me, her beautiful eyes following every inch of my body, was enough for me to harden beneath the towel. Thankfully, she left before she got a visual.

She was so flustered right before she fled; it made me laugh. At least I knew for sure I wasn't in this alone. I affected her as much as she affected me.

Saying she wanted to talk to me, though, instantly put me on edge. I knew what she was going to say, and the longer I stayed in my room, the longer it wasn't true. I thought for sure I was ready for her to leave, but as I stood there, still dripping water on the bedroom carpet, I realized I wasn't fully prepared.

I didn't want her to say the words.

I didn't want her to leave.

But only bad things would happen if she stayed. Call it a sixth sense, but I knew enough about her to know her innocent perception of the world would be shattered.

Throwing on a pair of sweatpants and a white T-shirt, I knew I had to get this over with. Or maybe I should walk down there in this towel. I wondered what she would have to say to me then. Would she be just as flustered? The thought was entertaining enough to make me smile as I walked into my office.

But it fell from my face when I saw her staring at one of the pictures hung on my wall. Her hands were folded behind her back, her long hair almost touching her fingers. She wore her typical black yoga pants and black T-shirt, but she looked so damn sexy the way she innocently swayed back and forth.

I rounded my desk and plopped down in the seat as soon as I was near, startling her away from the picture. "What did you want to talk to me about?" I asked, gathering the strength needed to prepare for our conversation.

"I know you gave me until today for my decision." She licked her lips, unaware of what she was doing to me.

"What decision?" I leaned back in my chair. I was being an ass, but I couldn't help myself.

"Whether or not I was going to move in here. You know, for the live-in maid position." She closed the distance between us, stopping only when her waist hit the edge of my desk. Our eyes locked on each other, like we were engaged in some sort of battle. She tried her hardest to give off the air of reservation, all while I tried not to snatch her up and throw her on the couch, demanding she let me inside her tight little body. Because she was standing in front of my desk, she couldn't see where my hand was. She would most definitely flee from my office if she knew I was touching myself, but I couldn't help it. I was reduced to a fucking hormone whenever she was around, and I found it rather unnerving.

"Well, what's your decision?" I readied myself for both elation and disappointment to come flooding over me.

"Okay." She placed her hand on her hip and stood before me in silence.

"Okay, what?" Confusion stole my good sense, my brain thrumming inside my head with a barrage of questions.

"I accept your terms of being your live-in maid." Her posture was rigid, her expression stoic and void of any sort of reservation. *What did she just say?*

No, no, no. That was not supposed to happen. She was supposed to yell and scream at me, let loose and tell me how much of an ass I'd been to her since the day she'd walked in with Beverly almost a month ago. She was supposed to tell me to go to hell and shove the job right up my ass.

She wasn't supposed to agree to live here.

With me.

Under this roof where we'll run into each other all the fucking time. My plan to get rid of this sweet creature blew up in my goddamn face. Fuck!

"Are you serious, Lila? You're going to accept my conditions? Why?" I asked, all reason and decorum leaving me. I was truly baffled, and I needed her to explain herself. First, she donned the ridiculous maid outfit I gave her initially, and now this? *What is wrong with this girl? Is she that desperate for a job?*

Or is she that desperate to be around me?

The thought made me smile, most likely making me look like some sort of crazy man right then, but I couldn't help the expression. *Yes, of course. That has to be it. She wants me and will do anything to be near me, even if it means bending to my most ludicrous of demands.*

Before she answered, I blurted, "Nothing can ever happen between us, you know. This relationship is strictly professional." I stood from my chair and took a few steps in her direction. "Do you understand me?"

She looked like I'd asked her the square root of a million,

her brows cinched together so tightly she'd give herself an instant headache if she didn't relax, and soon. Moments passed as my words fully sank in, and once they had, she took a tentative step back and inhaled a ragged breath of air. She looked offended, as if I had just told her to suck my dick. Not that I would've been opposed to such a thing.

Focus, man.

She appeared distraught, struggling to find the right words. Her face had become quite expressive, allowing me to guess at what she'd been thinking. She battled between blowing off my ludicrous statement and telling me exactly where she thought I could go.

"I don't want anything to happen between us either." She cringed. "Trust me," she exclaimed. She lied to us both, but I'd let it slide. This time. "I'm accepting this position because I need a job, and that's all there is to it."

"Who is going to take care of your mother then?" The words were out of my mouth before I could even think to stop them.

"How do you know about my mother?" She seemed troubled by my question, my invasion into her personal life seemingly too intimate.

"Beverly mentioned it to me. So, who is going to take care of her with you living here now?" If she wasn't going to come to her senses on her own, I'd be only too happy to give her a push. And if guilt was that card, then I'd gladly lay it on the table, exploiting the hell out of the emotion.

"I've made arrangements, so there is no need for you to worry." She continued to bite her tongue, and I found her control to be admirable. Stupid, but admirable.

Suddenly, I needed a drink. I brushed past her to pour one, looking back at her once more before lifting the decanter, all the while shaking my head back and forth.

She'd certainly thrown me for a loop. Not only had my plan

backfired, but I was going to have to try even harder to restrain myself whenever she was near. Then a disturbing thought rushed forward. She'd be sleeping just down the hall from me.

"Fine," I grunted, swallowing the amber liquid, allowing its burn to kick away my indecent thoughts. "Tomorrow night will be your first official night of living here." I waved my hand dismissively in the air between us. "We'll work out the details later on."

Why couldn't she have told me this at the end of the day, when I knew she'd be leaving, even if she *was* going to be coming back? But now, I was left to deal with all the disruptive thoughts and feelings exploding inside me.

She left my office in a huff, her hair whipping around her as she practically ran from the room. Of course, my sole focus was on her round ass as she hurried away from me. I needed to rein it all in if I wanted a shot of not completely going insane.

I could do this. I could treat her as just another employee.

A really hot, sensual, desirable employee.

Oh, who the fuck am I kidding?

Nothing good was going to come of this.

TWELVE
LILA

"NO, ABSOLUTELY NOT, Lila," my mother balked. "No daughter of mine is going to be living with some strange man. No." She was going to say more but instead started coughing, and I'd instantly felt guilty for making her physically upset. The only thing that would get her to stop was some of her favorite raspberry tea, plus placating the cause of her distress.

"Mom, I don't have a choice. I need the job. *We* need the job." I walked into the kitchen and put the teakettle on the stove. I wasn't going to give in, so I prayed the tea would do the trick all by itself.

"Lila, honey, I have to agree with Lillian here. It's not safe for a beautiful, young woman to be all alone with a strange man," my aunt agreed. She continued before I could get a word in. "Seriously, it's just not safe. You don't even know him. What if he's some kind of psycho? What would you do then?"

The two of them sat side by side on the couch, joining forces against me, all because I tried to do what was best for our family. Even though I knew their concern strictly came from love, it didn't lessen my annoyance. They were worried about me, but my physical well-being wasn't in question. It was my hormones and sanity that came to the forefront of my mind in terms of safety.

Once I heard the whistle of the kettle, I grabbed a cup from the counter rack and one raspberry tea bag. By the time I gave the drink to my mother, her coughing fit had all but ceased.

The flush painted on my mom's cheeks gave me hope she'd be okay. She just had to be. There'd be a lot of hard roads ahead, but I had every faith she'd pull through. And with some extra help, I could release some of the burden that had been stressing me out.

"How about if you meet him?" I blurted, the words leaving my mouth before my brain could filter out the nonsense. "Would you be okay with me living there then?"

"Yes," they chirped in unison, both dawning a satisfied smile.

I'd offered, so I had to follow through. But I couldn't bring both of them with me to my job to meet my boss, so I went for the lesser of two evils. If I brought my mom, she'd relentlessly interrogate Mr. Maxwell, and I didn't quite know how he'd react. He might fire me on the spot for the hassle. No, I had to bring Aunt Ellie with me. She wouldn't embarrass me. Well, not as much. Plus, she was closer to my age, only being ten years my senior. She'd be able to relate more to my situation.

"Okay," I agreed, but held my hand up to silence them before they interrupted. "But I'm taking Aunt Ellie to meet him. Not you," I said, pointing an accusing finger at the woman who gave me life. "You'll get me fired and you know it."

"I don't know what you're talking about, Lila." She might be sick, but the mama bear would come out to protect me. And it was that kind of protecting that would get me tossed right out the front door. As I stood there with my hands on my hips and my brows raised, she finally relented. "Fine. You can take Ellie."

I wasn't born yesterday. I knew she'd prep her with what questions to ask. I just hoped my aunt conveyed concern instead of crazy.

WE STOOD OUTSIDE the main entrance to his home when I suddenly became sick to my stomach. My nerves rattled me and I tried everything I could to calm myself before the door swung open.

Before I could rethink our agreement, my boss filled the doorway, his eyes quickly roving from me to my aunt and back again. I heard her sharp inhale right before she grabbed onto my arm, as if she needed to steady herself. I refused to look at her, though; my eyes focused solely on the man in front of me.

His eyebrows knit in confusion, but instead of explaining, I pushed past him as my shadow followed me.

"Lila, who is this? You know I don't like strangers in my home," he barked, rushing forward to catch up.

"Actually, I *don't* know that, Mr. Maxwell." I stared up at him, silently pleading with him not to be the ass I knew he could be. Not in front of my aunt. *All I need is for her to run home and tell my mom I'm working for a tyrant.* For this to work, I needed everyone to be on board with my decision, myself included.

"Well, we'll discuss the rules later on," he replied. Before I could say anything, he stepped forward and extended his hand to my aunt, the corners of his mouth tipping up into a genuine smile. "Hello, I'm Mason Maxwell. And you are . . . ?" he asked as he held tightly onto her hand.

I almost staggered backward. His immediate relaxation made him much more handsome, if that was even possible. While his focus wasn't on me, I surveyed him, noticing how enticing he looked in a pair of dark-washed jeans paired with a green, long-sleeved shirt, the fabric hugging every one of his toned muscles. His dark hair was tousled, as if he'd been running his hands through it, over and over again.

He is spectacular.

Aunt Ellie had been reduced to a pile of mush, her obvious attraction written all over her face. *Welcome to my world.* "I'm Ellie," she said, blatantly drinking him all in. It was only after I cleared my throat did she somewhat come back to her senses. "I'm Lila's aunt."

"Nice to meet you, Ellie." He took a step back and folded his arms over his chest. He continued to smile, but it faltered slightly when his gaze connected with mine. If I hadn't been memorizing his face, again, I wouldn't have even caught it. But I was, and I did. "Is there something I can do for you, Ellie?"

Silence stole her words. When I looked in her direction, I almost laughed aloud; she was practically drooling over him and it was rather amusing to witness. Don't get me wrong; I did the same thing, but I wasn't as obvious. *At least, I don't think I am.*

When she still didn't answer, I nudged her in the side.

"Oh, sorry. Mason, is it? The reason I'm here is to check you out." I started coughing, and she instantly corrected herself. "What I mean is, I'm here on behalf of Lila's family, to make sure the man she's going to be living under the same roof with is not some crazy psycho."

He chuckled before turning toward his office, waving us on to follow him. Once inside, we both took a seat on the leather couch while he made his way to his desk. He didn't sit down behind it, though. Leaning against the edge of it, he proceeded to cross his arms over his chest again. I'd been told it was a defensive stance, but he looked anything but. He actually appeared relaxed and forthcoming, which was weird to see.

"So, what would Lila's family like to know about me? Ask away." *Oh, shit!* I hadn't inquired about what she was going to ask him. I should've had her run them by me first. Holding my breath, I prayed she didn't embarrass me, not too much, at least.

"Let's start with, what do you do for a living? You obviously do well for yourself here. You're not into anything illegal, are you?" My eyes went wide at her question. *I think I'm going to die right here and now.*

But instead of him being offended and tossing us both out the door, he simply laughed. Again. "No, I'm not into anything illegal," he answered, his fingers tightening around his biceps. "I made my money years ago in the stock market, and now I manage a large investment portfolio." His words were precise, his tone telling her he wasn't going to elaborate. He came across polite but silently warned her not to push. I wasn't sure she caught on, probably still too in awe of him to detect even the slightest inflection in his voice.

"Okay. Second question," she rattled.

"Don't you mean third question?" His lips were still curved upward, but he was losing some of his patience.

"Yes, I guess you're right." She leaned forward and asked the most embarrassing question. "What are your intentions with our Lila?" Once her question hit the air, she leaned back and crossed her own arms over her chest, clearly satisfied with unnerving everyone in the room.

"My intentions with *your* Lila are strictly of a professional nature. She's my employee, and I'm her employer. That's all there is to it. My home is large and I now require someone on a full-time, permanent basis to keep up with it. She's being paid well, and she'll have every comfort available." He circled his desk and took a seat, clicking on the computer screen. I knew what that meant. It was his dismissive move, and I wanted to get my aunt out of there before she witnessed *that* guy.

He continued to make eye contact with her, but his mood was not as light as it had been five minutes before.

"All right, well, I'm satisfied. Thank you for your time, Mason." She stood and approached him. He stood as well and accepted her outstretched hand. "It was nice to meet you."

"The pleasure was all mine, Ellie. Lila will see you out now. She does have some work to get to." We were almost out of his office when he instructed, "Lila, stop by and see me before you start your duties."

I nodded and walked my aunt outside, my chest tight in anticipation of what he was going to say.

We were standing by the driver side of her car, when she blurted, "Holy shit, Lila. You never mentioned your new boss looks like that! I just about humped his leg once he smiled at me." She laughed as she opened her door.

"Aunt Ellie!" I exasperated. To be honest, I was used to the things she said, although that time, it really had taken me a bit by surprise. Maybe it was because we shared the same thoughts about him.

"I like him."

"I'm sure you do." I leaned in and gave her a hug before she took off down the long driveway, leaving me all alone to wonder what exactly he wanted to talk to me about this time.

THIRTEEN
MASON

WHAT WAS SHE *fucking thinking bringing someone to my house?* I tried to calm myself before she came back inside, because if not, I was going to explode. For as much as I didn't like the situation, however, I knew it wasn't her fault. I could understand her family being concerned. And I could appreciate her having people who would step up and make sure she was being safe. She was luckier than most.

But it was the perfect opportunity to go over the list of rules I'd put together. Luckily, I'd been jotting them down so when I gave her the complete list, she couldn't say she wasn't warned when she disobeyed one of them.

If she wants to be here, with me, in this house, then she must comply.

Initially, I was admittedly being a jerk when I started the list of rules, but the further along I went, the more I realized it was for her safety as well as mine.

Lila strode back into my office, fidgeting with the hem of her shirt, trying to look me in the eye but faltering every now and again. I made her nervous, and the thought elated me, mostly because she unnerved me as well.

"What did you want to talk to me about?" She dropped her

hands to her sides and waited.

"I wanted to give you a list of rules you're to follow while in my employment. It's short, but I reserve the right to add to it at any time." I motioned for her to approach, and when she was near, I extended the piece of paper to her. "Give them a read."

She accepted the paper and started to turn around to leave. I cleared my throat, signaling I wanted her to face me. She did. "What?" she asked innocently.

"Read them here. In front of me. Aloud."

"What?" Clearly, she was confused. "You want me to read them to you?"

"Yes. Plus, if you have any issues or questions, we can deal with it right here and now."

She glanced around briefly before bringing the list up in front of her. Exhaling a frustrated breath, she began.

"*There will be no unapproved visitors. You will receive a key to the house, but if you lose this key, you will not receive another. If this happens, you will have to work around my schedule in order for you to come and go. You will have your own private quarters, equipped with your own bathroom.*" She stopped and took a breath before reading the last rule. "*There will be a strict curfew of eight o'clock. You will work Monday through Friday, having both Saturday and Sunday off, but again, you will be in the house by eight o'clock.*" She abruptly stopped reading and stared at me, mouth wide open. "You can't be serious. I have a curfew? I'm not a child. You can't make me follow this, especially on the weekends."

"I can, and I will." The look on my face was serious. She might push back on the rules later, but at that moment, she remained silent. Physically, though, her body vibrated with anger. The paper shook in her hands and she looked like she was ready to lunge across the desk at me.

After a very long minute, she relaxed. "Is that all?" she asked, sarcasm dripping from those three words.

"For now, it is. You may go." I gave her one of my flippant hand waves, and she was out the door before I could even blink.

THERE ARE SO many of them. They're all around me, reaching out and begging me to help them. But I can't. I can't help them all. As I walk down the long, dank corridor, my heart skips countless beats before it threatens to stop altogether. I find myself holding what little breath I have left until I come upon the room I was sent to.

Turning the handle very slowly, praying I walk into nothing, I push the large wooden door open until I can see a bed in the center of the room. As I move in closer, I see what it is I was sent in here for.

There's a girl lying on the mattress, and I'm not sure she's even alive. My feet inch forward until I'm standing at the edge, my hand reaching out to touch her skin. She's restrained. Her hands are tied at the wrists to each corner of the headboard, and her feet are secured much the same way to the footboard.

She's naked.

I take in my next breath, but it escapes me quickly as I'm shoved forward. I fall next to her still form and am instantly frozen.

Why am I here?

Why are they making me do this? I want to scream, but no sound escapes. I want to cry, but I can't show weakness. If I show any fragility, they will do to me what they do to them.

Them.

There are so many . . . of them.

I woke up covered in a sheen of sweat. *Fuck! I haven't had that dream in a very long time.* Pissed it had started up again, I threw the covers off me and stalked toward the bathroom, intent on scrubbing myself clean. I'd thought I was past that stage of the fear. It had happened years before, yet it felt like it had only been a day.

After my shower, I threw on some clothes before heading downstairs to grab a stiff drink. It was the only thing that would put me back to sleep, the alcohol numbing the pain, giving me the escape my soul craved.

An hour later, and I was no closer to sleep, but I *was* closer to oblivion. The scotch kicked my ass, and it took every muscle in my body to work in unison when I stood up so I didn't face-plant onto the floor. Slowly staggering out of my office, down the hall, and toward the kitchen, I took notice of the light ahead of me. Normally, the house was pitch-black. No one there but me. Then it dawned on me I was not the only person living under my roof anymore.

She's *here now.*

I tried to be quiet and stealthy as I walked toward the source of the brightness, not knowing if I'd find her in there or not. She could've left the light on when she retired for the evening.

I knew she was upset with me about the list of rules earlier. She probably thought I was just being an ass, as usual, but little did she know they were necessary.

As I approached the entryway, I saw her. She wasn't aware of me just yet, but if my body didn't start to cooperate soon, she would.

Covering her delectable body was a thin pink tank top and loose pajama bottoms. Thought after dirty thought filtered in, and I smiled at the fantasy of ripping away those scraps of material. When she bent over in front of the fridge, scouring to find something to eat, I almost lost it. I knew she had found what she was looking for when she opened the freezer, let out a little squeal of delight, and reached for the peanut butter brittle ice cream I kept in there at all times.

What can I say? It's my weakness.

Moving silently across the floor, my presence was still

undetected. As I was about to reach out and touch her, for whatever reason I wasn't sure, she turned around and her body crashed into mine. She twitched in fear until she realized it was only me, and then she reacted much like the way I thought she would. Even drunk, I was aware of the effect I had on her.

"Mr. Maxwell, you scared me," she yelped. She backed up a few paces until there was a professional space between us, but it was too late. She was already ingrained inside me by then. I inhaled her scent and it instantly made me hard as fuck. Her hair was damp, so I knew she had recently showered, the image making me ache in places I hadn't even known existed. I imagined her hands running all over her wet, soapy body, pinching and squeezing her taunting flesh. Then I was in the fantasy with her, my hands taking over and disappearing inside her, making her moan my name under the fitful spray of the water.

The clank of a bowl and spoon tore me from my drunken thoughts. She scooped out some of my ice cream with a gentle smile on her beautiful lips.

"You know that's mine, don't you?" I slurred, a little more than I'd wanted. *Damn it! I'm drunker than I was two minutes ago.*

Turning her head so her eyes landed on my face, she smiled even more and brought the spoon to her mouth. Her tongue shot out and she licked the side of it, the ice cream dripping back into the bowl.

"Is this another rule? I'm not allowed to eat your ice cream?" Her tone indicated she was annoyed, yet there was a hint of playfulness to her voice. Or maybe there wasn't. I was drunk, after all.

I reached forward and tried to snatch it from her, but she was too quick. Or maybe I was too slow. She held the bowl in front of her as she walked backward, taking small bites, playing with me the entire time. She was teasing me with my ice cream, thinking I wanted to have it for myself. What she didn't realize was I wanted to eat her up instead.

"Lila, stop it," I barked.

"Stop what? Eating your precious ice cream? Technically, it's not in the rules, so I'm not disobeying."

"Stop tormenting me, damn it."

Suddenly, she stopped. Placing the bowl on the countertop, she retreated until her back hit the wall. She was trapped. I stole the distance between our bodies in a few short strides and crowded her personal space, glaring down at her like she'd been torturing me on purpose.

I was but a breath away from her lips when she spoke. "What are you doing?" she asked nervously.

"I'm doing what I should have done the first time you walked into my office. Into my life. I'm going to taste you."

Her breath caught in her throat as I leaned in closer. "Mr. Maxwell—"

"Call me Mason," I instructed, leaning even closer still. "I want to hear my name on your lips."

She didn't know what else to do, so she whispered, "Mason," back at me, and whatever reserve I'd been holding onto flew right out the motherfucking window. I crashed my lips against hers, and I wasn't gentle. My need for her was dangerously too much as I bit at her lower lip until she opened up for me. When she did, and my tongue played with hers, it was all too consuming.

With one hand on the side of her face and the other snaked around her waist, I pulled her to me, securing her in place.

"Why are you doing this to me?" I never waited for her answer, instead continuing to ravage her mouth. But when I gripped underneath her ass and lifted her on top of the counter, spread her legs wide, and stepped between them, she tensed before breaking the connection.

Her hands were on my chest, and it took me a few seconds

to realize she was trying to push me away. Drunk or not, I'd never force her. Reluctantly, I pulled back.

"I can't do this. *We* can't do this," she mumbled before shoving me back. And because of the alcohol, I stumbled enough for her to hop off the counter and hurry from the kitchen, running away from me as quickly as possible.

What did I just do?

FOURTEEN
LILA

THREE WEEKS HAD passed since he'd kissed me in the kitchen. Three weeks since a part of my fantasy had come true. Three weeks since I could've kicked myself for stopping him, but I knew I didn't want anything to happen while he was not in his right mind, if ever at all. My head told me to stay away from him. Too bad my hormones appeared to be stronger than reason.

That night, however, I wasn't going to dwell on the very complicated, very confusing, Mr. Mason Maxwell. Instead, my dear friend Eve and I were going out for dinner and drinks. I didn't normally drink, mainly because I didn't like anything altering my state of mind, but after living with a man who confused me, both mentally and physically, I needed to partake in some alcohol.

It was three in the afternoon and I'd finished all my assigned duties for the day. I knew I didn't want to rock the boat and have him scold me like some sort of child, so I told Eve we had to plan an early evening: dinner at four with the much-needed drinks to follow.

Making my way toward his office, I planned on getting his approval for her to pick me up at the house. There was no way I was inviting her inside though; I liked her way too much to subject her to the likes of my mercurial boss.

I found him sifting through his desk drawer, a look of confusion plastered across his features certainly a sight to see. Normally, the man was in full control of everything around him and everything had its place, so to see him in a state of disarray was odd.

When I cleared my throat, he slammed the drawer shut and cursed under his breath. Then his head whipped up in my direction, clearly not a happy camper.

"Sorry to interrupt, but I was wondering if it was okay if my friend picked me up, here at the house." I fidgeted, shuffling my feet back and forth and moving side to side.

"No" was all he said, turning his attention back toward the pile of papers on his desk.

I'd put up with enough from him during my employment, even his drunken kiss, which he never talked about after that night.

Enough is enough.

"No?" I asked, the inflection in my tone rising.

"No," he repeated, more definitive. "I don't want strangers in my house, Lila. You know this."

"She's not a stranger. She's my best friend."

"She's a stranger to me." He marched toward the bookshelf, clearly still looking for something. With each movement he made, I could feel my temper starting to rise, but for the sake of my job, I tried my very best to not lash out. Getting into an argument right then wouldn't have done either one of us any good, especially since the tension between us was as thick as ever.

I backed up until I hovered between his office and the grand foyer. "I never intended for Eve to come inside your precious house," I said a little too sarcastically. He flinched at my brazenness. "She's going to pick me up outside at four o'clock." I turned my back to him, but before I disappeared, I blurted the last of my words over my shoulder. "And don't worry, I'll be back by curfew."

With ten minutes to spare before Eve arrived, I walked from my bedroom and strolled toward the stairs. I wasn't paying attention, busy looking inside my clutch to make sure I had money and my license, when a firm grip stopped me in my tracks.

I squealed.

I actually squealed in surprise.

When I looked up, I saw Mason glaring down at me. His dark eyes roved over my body, taking me in from head to toe. The kelly-green dress I bought a few months before was cut lower in the front than what I was used to, but since I was small chested, I wasn't spilling over the top. The material molded to my curves, making me feel pretty. I'd styled my hair in large waves, the red strands bouncing from side to side as I walked. I kept my makeup minimal since I favored the natural look.

"You're not actually going to wear that dress outside this house, are you?" His words were simple enough, but the tone behind them deemed possession. He acted like a jealous boyfriend, and I found it both irritating and oddly welcoming.

"Why do you care what I wear when I'm off the clock?" I didn't know how else to respond, his interest in me surprising. After all, he seemed to be avoiding me since he cornered me in the kitchen. I didn't want to indulge his craziness, but I was curious to find out why he even cared.

"You're never really off the clock, Lila, and you would do well to remember that. Just because I allow you to come and go doesn't mean I'm not aware of everything you do." He stopped speaking almost as quickly as he had started, averting his eyes from mine.

Again, his words struck me as odd, but Eve was going to be there any second and I wanted to get the hell out of the house as soon as possible. I had never wanted, or needed, a drink as much as I did right then.

I didn't respond, instead shrugging my arm from his hand.

He didn't let me go at first, but after I tried to break away a second time, he relented and finally released me. Taking a few steps to the side, he allowed me to pass and descend the stairwell. I didn't look behind me, but I felt his eyes all over me. I knew he was watching me, taking in every sway of my hips, every step my toned legs took.

I decided it was better for me to wait outside for Eve than to remain in his presence one more second, so I walked out the front door. Luckily, she was right on time, and as soon as she stopped the car, I hopped in and slammed the door. She didn't move at first, and I looked over to see what the problem was.

"Is that your freaking boss, Lila?" I turned my head toward the house and, sure enough, he was standing in the open doorway, continuing to glare at me. "Holy shit, girl. He's amazing."

"He's an ass," I retorted, stealing back my attention from him. "Can we go now?" I prayed she'd come back to reality and step on the gas pedal, driving us further away from his intense gaze.

"He can be an ass to me any time he wants," she laughed, steering the car away from the house.

EVE AND I hadn't been able to connect in the past couple weeks, mainly because of our jobs. She worked late hours at the law firm where she was employed; she was studying to be a lawyer but was working as a legal assistant. And I still went home every day to spend some time with my mom and Aunt Ellie. So I was happy we were able to meet up that night.

We chose La Costa's, because they had the best Mexican food around, and we gorged ourselves until we were full. Since the restaurant had a nice bar, we decided to stay and have a few drinks instead of traveling somewhere else, saving both time and energy.

Energy we reserved for drinking.

"Did I tell you the latest with my mother?" Eve asked before reaching for her drink.

"Oh, God, what now?" I had never wished death on anyone, and I wasn't going to start right then. However, I hoped her mother would up and disappear. Mental issues or not, she was a rotten woman who didn't deserve to *talk* to someone like Eve, let alone claim to be her mother. Which she wasn't, not by any stretch of the imagination.

"She called me the other day, ranting and raving how it was my fault she was alone. She said I took everyone from her life, and I was going to rot in hell for it." She downed the rest of her cranberry and vodka and motioned to the bartender.

"Why do you take her calls? You should just cut all ties. She's nothing but poison. She's the one who is going to rot in hell for treating you this way." I think I was quite possibly angrier than she was. Maybe it was because she was used to dealing with her; I wasn't sure. But whatever the reason, someone was holding a spot in heaven for my friend.

"I don't take them often, trust me. But she *is* my mother, and I know she's sick. So I let her rant and rave and then she's good for a month or so. I know everything she says is crazy. I know what happened to my brother and my father wasn't my fault. I know this, so it doesn't bother me when she says it is." When the bartender came closer, she asked for a soda.

"What, only one drink tonight? I thought we were going to let loose."

"Well, since I'm driving, it's probably not the best thing to be drinking. One is good for me anyway. But drink up." She smiled, but the look on her face told me something was bothering her. Turning on her stool to face me, she put her hand on my forearm and spoke. "Why *are* you drinking? Is it because of that hot-ass boss of yours?" She laughed, but little did she know she'd hit the nail on the freaking head.

"I'd rather talk about your mother," I blurted, fully meaning every word.

"Holy shit, girl! It's that bad?"

"You have no idea, Eve." I took a large sip of my drink. "You have no idea," I repeated.

I filled my best friend in on everything, including the kiss. Trying to explain my feelings toward him, when even *I* didn't understand them, was almost impossible.

We ended up staying at the bar until nine, a full hour after I was supposed to be back at the house. But I was feeling a little more than tipsy and I wasn't thinking about what would happen once I got there.

Nothing was going to ruin my good mood.

Or so I thought.

I WAVED GOODBYE to my friend when she finally dropped me off, almost losing my balance and finding it rather amusing.

Stumbling up the front steps, I thankfully made it to the door. Because of my impaired vision, I struggled to find my key, cursing out loud at the inconvenience of it all.

All I needed to do was get into the damn house, go to my room, and pass out for the night. Oh, and try to avoid my boss in the process. I could only hope he'd gone out for the evening. He did that from time to time and was sometimes gone for the entire night, coming home in the early morning hours. But I'd never seen him when he returned home. He'd always somehow managed to slink off toward either his bedroom or that damn room he kept locked.

While I was still fumbling with my clutch, the door swung open and an opposing presence blocked my entrance. For some unknown reason, I started laughing, and the longer we stood there, the more I laughed. I wasn't sure if it was nerves or the fact I didn't care what he said to me or how he felt about me being late.

Alcohol will do that to a person.

"Are you fucking drunk?" he growled, leaning in closer to my personal space.

What gave it away? The uncontrollable laughter, or the fact I can hardly keep my balance? Maybe it was the smell of liquor emanating from me. Or no, wait, maybe it was the way my words were jumbled, falling from my lips.

"What? Wh . . . what did you shay?" I slurred, gripping the doorframe to balance myself.

He gripped my arms to steady me before I face-planted on the concrete steps. My head lolled around on top of my shoulders, making me feel like a newborn baby with no control of my movements. "Never mind. I can clearly tell you've had way too much to drink. Never again. Do you hear me?" he shouted, shaking me until I looked up at him. Geesh, I was drunk, not deaf.

The intoxicated me was braver than the sober me. Somehow, I managed to break away from him and push past him into the foyer. Whipping around, almost too fast, I steadied myself and loudly spoke. "You can't tell me what to do. I'll strink ever I want to do." I could hear the words coming out of my mouth, and I knew they were wrong, but I thought he could still understand me. I swayed a bit more, and as I turned around, my right foot not going with the rest of my body, I started to fall forward. But I never hit the ground.

Instead, a strong arm circled my waist, holding me upright. Then I felt warm, sweet breath on the side of my face. Inhaling, I closed my eyes and imagined feeling that same breath on my lips, imagining what his mouth would taste like again.

"Jesus Christ," he grunted. "Let's get you up to bed before you hurt yourself." He carried me up the stairs, down the hall, and into my bedroom. He didn't go straight to the bed, though. He walked me toward the chair in the corner of the room. "Sit," he fumed, his tone growing more and more impatient.

He bent down in front of me and grabbed my left leg. Slowly unstrapping my heel, he pulled it off and tossed it to the side. Then he moved to my right leg, repeating the task. Once my feet were bare, he helped me to stand, his hand immediately going to the side of my dress. When he started to unzip it, I closed my eyes and licked my lips. I had pictured him undressing me a million times before; I'd just never thought it would really happen. I lurched forward and threw my arms around him, pulling him into me.

"Don't you want me?" I asked as he tried to keep me steady, once again. Closing my eyes, I whispered, "I want to feel your lips on mine. I *need* to taste you again."

"Christ," I heard him mutter, before he unhooked my interlocked fingers from around his neck.

When I opened my eyes, not sure what to expect, he was simply looking at me. His face beautiful, yet expressionless. He captured his bottom lip between his teeth, teasing me more than he probably realized. I made a move toward him again, which made him speak up.

"Lila, stop it. Right now. Nothing is going to happen. I was drunk when I made that mistake, and I refuse to let you make the same one." His fingers fixated on my zipper once again, finally successful in getting it down.

"Why are you undressing me then? Huh? Tell me that, slicko."

"Slicko?" A faint smile appeared on his face. "Slicko," he repeated, more to himself than anything. "And to answer your question, I'm undressing you because I'm trying to put you to bed. Now stop fidgeting, and let me do this before you pass out and make it even harder."

His words spurred me to act in a way I'd never do had the alcohol not been coursing through my blood. Without another thought, my hand shot out and I ran my palm over the crotch of his pants, clearly feeling for his reaction to me.

And there it was.

Plain as day.

He was already at full length, hard and rigid against my fingers.

"Fuck me," he groaned, pushing my hand away from his arousal. "Stop doing that unless you want me to put you on your back." He grabbed my jaw and lifted my head. "Are you going to spread your legs for me, Lila?" His breath tickled my lips and I parted them in anticipation he would accept my brazenness and close the deal.

"Yes, it's what I want. Please," I begged him. I knew what I was saying, and I was allowing my inebriated state to take the courage to tell him. I would never have said those things to him sober, and we both knew it.

He roughly shook his head and within seconds his demeanor changed back to what it had been before: annoyed. "Stop moving around so I can help you."

I pushed his hands away, clearly agitated myself. "I don't need your damn shit," I slurred once again. He'd already accomplished the hardest part. The zipper was undone; all I had to do was pull off the dress and toss it across the room. A feat easier said than done.

Struggling to get the material over my head, I was sure I was quite the sight. But again, I didn't care what I looked like. My only objective was ridding myself of the damn thing.

"Here, let me get that for you," he offered, reaching out to help me once more. The fight in me waned, so I gave in. Once my dress was tossed to the floor, I stood in front of him in nothing but my red lace bra and matching panties. Normally, under any other circumstance, I would've been mortified. But that night, all my reservations had disappeared.

Standing there practically naked, I felt oddly empowered. I felt sexy. I felt wanted. Even if those feelings were false, I wanted to revel in them.

I sauntered toward him one more time, unhooking my bra in the process and tossing the scrap of lace to the floor to join my dress. I heard him inhale a breath and I smiled. "Do you like what you see, *Mason?*" I asked, my hands palming my breasts, teasing my nipples until the pink buds became erect. I took a few more steps before I stopped, removed my panties, and kicked them away from me. His fists clenched at his sides while the tic of his jaw was prominent.

He looked like he was about to lose it.

"What are you fucking trying to do to me? I'm struggling to do the right thing here, and you keep making it harder for me!"

"Oh, it's hard all right," I teased, right before reaching my hand out again to cup him. But I never made contact. He gripped my wrist and dragged me toward the bed.

"Finally!" I exclaimed. "I've been waiting for this ever since you kissed me." He didn't say anything before he pushed me onto the mattress. Instantly and clumsily, I shot up on all fours and turned to face him. My hair fell in front of me, covering my breasts, but I knew he could still see the rest of me. The ache that had been building between my legs was almost unbearable by that point. I needed some relief, and I wanted it to come in the form of his thick cock.

He stood frozen by the side of the bed. Our eyes were locked, but neither one of us did or said anything. I was slowly starting to sober up, and it had everything to do with the look of desire in his beautiful, dark eyes. I crawled to the edge, rose to my knees, and put my hands on his chest. His heart rammed against his ribs, just underneath the pads of my fingers.

Still, he didn't move.

I leaned in close, my lips twitching for his taste. I leaned in farther still, and our lips were but a single gasp away from each other. We stayed in that position for what seemed like forever, when in reality it was but a few seconds. I couldn't take it any longer. I demolished the last bit of distance between us and pressed my mouth to his. I was thirsty, and all I wanted was to drink him in. I teased him, tormented him, until he opened up for me and I latched on to his warmth. Our tongues tasted each other and the kiss became frenzied. He snaked his arms around me and pulled me into him. The groan that exploded from deep in his throat was enough to drench me, make me crazy with the need to have him.

He broke our kiss only to nibble at my flesh, making his way from my jawline to my neck and up to my sensitive lobe. "I want nothing more than to claim you, Lila, but I can't. *We* can't." He threw my words back at me, repeating what I'd told him in the kitchen all those weeks before, dispelling any notion of this happening. "It would be a mistake of epic proportions."

He moved back toward my mouth, placed a chaste kiss upon my lips, and then released me. I fell back on top of the covers. I should've been angry. I should've felt rejected. But all I could do was be elated from his touch, his taste as delicious as I remembered.

Intoxicating even.

Which was funny, because so was I.

Intoxicated.

A rumble started in my throat and soon burst forth from my mouth. I started laughing all over again; I couldn't help it.

"All right. All right. Let's get you into bed now." He pushed the covers back and helped me crawl under them. Once I was securely snuggled in, he covered me back up. My laughter had stopped by that point, exhaustion quickly taking over. I struggled to keep my eyes open.

Before they shut completely, I saw him lean over me then felt his lips brush my forehead.

Then I passed out cold.

FIFTEEN
MASON

THANK GOD IT was Saturday, which meant Lila wouldn't be working with a nasty hangover. I didn't have to worry about her breaking some of my expensive shit because she couldn't function properly.

Looking down at my phone as it rang, I noticed it was the one number I never wanted to answer. Deciding it was best to ignore the call, I made my way into the kitchen to grab a bottle of water. Once upstairs, I stopped off in my bathroom to grab some headache medication. The good shit.

Approaching her bedroom, I didn't even bother knocking, convinced she was still sound asleep. It was only eight in the morning, after all. But instead, I was shocked to find her sitting up in bed, her eyes on me as soon as I stepped into her space. She held the covers tightly under her chin, clearly realizing she was fully naked. I knew she had some questions about the night before; I could see it written all over her face.

"How are you feeling?" I asked, moving toward her. "I brought you something for your head. And make sure you drink the entire bottle of water. You are, no doubt, dehydrated."

I handed her both items and stood there until she did as I

commanded. When she was finished, she lay back down and closed her eyes, but not before her hand flew to her temple.

"What happened last night? I feel awful. I don't think I've ever felt this bad before in my entire life." A whimper escaped her lips and I actually felt sorry for her.

I hadn't put myself in that type of situation in a very long time, but I remembered the feeling. It was exactly why I didn't get rip-roaring drunk anymore. *Well, other than a few weeks ago.* But I had an excuse then. It was a shitty excuse, but it was an excuse nonetheless. She had me so twisted up inside myself the only thing that would give me an ounce of reprieve was a drink . . . or two . . . or five.

"You apparently got a little wasted," I chastised, holding my thumb and index finger up close together. "Do you remember anything after you came here?" I was hoping she did, just as much as I was hoping she didn't. Either way had me working out different scenarios in my head.

If she *did* recall everything, especially in her bedroom, then we'd have to sit down and hash it all out. I'd have to dispel any notions she had toward me and guarantee her in return I wouldn't act on anything either. I knew she wasn't stupid. I knew she was aware I desired her; I was shit at subtlety.

Of course, the better option would be if she didn't remember. Which meant our talk would happen sometime in the future. A part of me wanted to get it over with here and now, though. Only so I wouldn't have to think about it again.

"I remember Eve dropping me off. She thinks you're hot, by the way. But I had to dash her image of you by letting her in on a little secret." Her eyelids were still closed, shielding her from my expressions. She knew me enough already to know what she was doing was going to let her say anything she wanted, within reason, and she wouldn't be interrupted by the scowl that was sure to take up residence on my face.

"And what, pray tell, secret is that?" I asked, eager to learn the answer even though I could guess. It wasn't rocket science what she thought of me. Thought, not felt. Because I knew she felt things for me, things she wouldn't fully act on. Not unless, of course, she had some liquid courage swirling around inside her.

"That while you might be spectacular to look at, you're not very nice." After her declaration, she threw her entire arm over her eyes, shielding out even more of the little bit of light that crept through her window.

I couldn't help but smile. Although she'd insulted me, I loved that she thought me to be spectacular to look at. Even though nothing could happen between us anymore, the idea she liked what she saw boosted my ego that much more. I was fully aware of the reaction I obtained from women, but hers was the only one I cared about.

Several minutes of silence passed while neither one of us spoke. I carefully contemplated my next words, waiting for her to open her eyes. She ended up speaking first. "Is it okay if I go back to sleep?"

"It's your day off. You can do anything you want." I couldn't keep the raspy desire from my voice, no matter how hard I tried. It didn't escape my attention she was stark naked under those covers, and the more I thought about it, the more my body reacted. Knowing we were both in danger of repeating a dangerous mistake, I turned on my heel and made my way out of her room, grabbing my pants to settle the big guy down.

As I distracted myself with work, my cell rang, vibrating against the top of my desk and making twice the amount of noise. He was calling me again, but I didn't want to have to deal with him, so I let the call ring out, but it started up again, and again, and again. *Persistent bastard.*

Blowing out a pent-up breath, I pressed the answer key and shouted into the phone. "What!"

"What the fuck, Maxwell? You better answer every time I call, you got that? Or do I have to remind you of what could happen?" His threat came through loud and clear.

"No," I gritted. "You don't have to remind me." I steadied my breathing before continuing. "What do you want?"

"I have a job for you, of course. Why else would I call you? To chat?" He laughed at his own stupid little joke. *How I want to kill this fucker. All in due time, I guess.*

"I can't do it. I'm busy." I knew he wasn't going to accept my excuse, but I gave it anyway. "Can't you get someone else?"

"You act like you don't get paid for your services. And paid handsomely, I might add. You know I don't want anyone else involved. Too much risk. No, I much prefer your services, *Dr.* Maxwell," he goaded.

"I'm not a fucking doctor and you know it."

"You're *my* goddamn doctor and that's all that matters. Now, stop fucking around. I'll text you the address, and I expect you to be there within the hour." I knew he had me by the balls and there wasn't a damn thing I could do about it.

Esteban Frontera was one of the most powerful, evil men I'd ever had the displeasure of knowing. Normally, someone so high up in his *organization* wouldn't be the one reaching out, making calls and finding someone to do his lowly bidding. But since he had a hard-on for me, he made sure to be my only point of contact.

When silence continued to be my only response, he said something that sent chills right through me. "Don't make me come to you, Mason. You don't want that."

There was no more hesitation on my part; there was no way he was coming anywhere near my private life. "I'll be there."

"Good boy," he said, before hanging up.

THE JOB TOOK me longer than the last. The location was only forty-five minutes away, but the security was more rigorous. It took me a half hour before they even let me in. Needless to say, I was a little more than pissed off. I just wanted to get in, shut off all emotions, and get out.

Pulling up in front of my house, I noticed Lila's car was still there. *Shit!* Normally, I didn't get called out so early in the morning. Typically, it was late at night, when the rest of the world was fast asleep. Everyone except the criminals I dealt with.

It was almost noon; there was no way she was still sleeping. I was sure by that point she was up roaming through the whole house, making it much more difficult to slink off to my room to clean up.

Opening the door slightly, I looked around cautiously as if I were a burglar breaking into the place. When I didn't immediately see Lila, I entered my own damn home and instantly made my way upstairs. I took out my keys and unlocked the one room in the house I kept off-limits from everyone. I placed my black bag inside, jotted down some notes, and left quickly, making sure to lock the door behind me.

As I was about to turn around and head toward my bedroom, I stopped short. Lila was there, standing directly behind me. I could feel her presence. I could sense the trepidation emanating from her.

I instantly tensed up, all the muscles in my back as rigid as could be. "Are you okay?" she asked.

Was I okay? No, I most certainly was not. I was being black-mailed into something the devil himself might turn down. I was living with a woman who tempted my very soul every time I laid eyes on her. Shit, every time I even thought about her.

No, I was far from okay.

But I couldn't let her know that, so I gave her the answer that would hopefully get her to leave me alone. "Yeah, just need a shower." I turned toward her and started walking down the hallway until her sound of surprise made me stop dead in my tracks.

"Oh my God! You're bleeding." She closed the short distance in mere seconds as her hands flew to my chest. Catching me totally off-guard, she didn't allow me the time to react as I should have. I *should* have pushed past her and hurried toward my bedroom, but her touch froze me in place.

I'd completely forgotten about the blood on my shirt. I was usually very careful not to be seen that way, for fear of something like this happening. There was no excuse I could come up with fast enough to placate her growing concern.

"I'm fine, Lila. Really." It was the only response that came to mind.

"What happened? Were you in an accident? Did you get into a fight? Is that even your blood?" She fired question after question at me, and it quickly made my mood go from sour to borderline explosive. I wasn't used to having someone all up in my business like that. Beverly and Norma knew enough to keep out of my personal affairs. Although, neither one of them had ever seen me with blood on my clothes before. I could kick myself for being so careless. If truth be told, all I could think about on the way home was her. And it was because of her I was in my foul-ass mood.

"I'm fine," I barked, making a move to brush past her, but she grabbed my wrist to stop me. "What are you doing, woman?" My temper evident on my face, in my voice, and in my body language, I was prepared to fight if that was what it came down to. Not physically, of course, but verbally. Anything to get her to leave me alone.

"You can talk to me, you know. I'm a pretty good listener."

She flashed me a timid smile.

While I appreciated the offer, more than she would ever know, this was exactly what I was trying to avoid. I couldn't have that type of relationship with her. Not at all. Too many bad things happened when there weren't clear-cut boundaries.

I yanked my wrist from her delicate hand and stalked past her, continuing on down the hallway. "You would do best to keep your nose out of my business!" I yelled over my shoulder, right before I slammed my bedroom door.

I didn't see her for the rest of the day; she'd left soon after our little encounter. I assumed she went to visit her mother, but I didn't know for sure. All I cared about was she wasn't sharing the same space with me for the moment. I needed to get my head right. And I needed to make sure I was more careful in the future.

I went to bed early, but not until after I knew Lila had returned for the evening. As I drifted off to sleep, the only thought I had bouncing around in my head was of her. The woman who was slowly, but surely, binding herself into every cell in my body.

AS I ADVANCE toward the tied-up girl, my stomach is in danger of revolting against me. I know exactly what I'm supposed to do, and the dire consequences of not following through will be dreadful.

Frontera grabs my shoulder and whips me around so I'm facing his disgusting face. He jams something in my hand. "Make sure to wear this. You don't want to catch something from these putas." He glares at me, the scar on his right cheek jumping in the light. "Plus, there's nothing worse than a pregnant puta. Because a pregnant puta is a worthless puta."

I don't know how I'm not punching him in the face right now. Oh, yeah, I know why. Because he has someone watching my sister. That's why. If I don't do exactly what he wants, when he wants, then I can say goodbye to ever seeing her alive again.

"You better do it, pendejo," he whispers in my ear. "You better fuck her real good. Let her know who's boss."

He crowds me, his excitement evident in everything he does, from the way he watches me, to the tone in his creepy voice. He nudges me none too lightly toward the woman splayed out on the bed. As I get closer, I hear her whimpers. I sense her fear, and it makes me want to kill everyone here.

But I have to do this if I expect to get out of here alive. When I'm close enough, I reach out to touch her. I'm trying to be gentle, trying to let her know I don't mean to hurt her, that this isn't my choice. And as I'm about to climb onto the bed, she turns her head toward me and locks eyes with me.

All I can see are those beautiful, soul-scorching green eyes.

Her eyes.

Lila's eyes.

I awoke with a start, drenched from my nightmare. And I knew if I wanted them to end, I had to make a decision and make it soon.

SIXTEEN
LILA

WHEN I SAW the blood on his shirt, I about had a heart attack, my inner voice screaming at me to pay attention. There was something going on with him, yet I had no idea what it was. But I had to find out. Or I had to at least try. He was so closed off, and I couldn't talk to Beverly or Norma about him, because their loyalty surely lay with him. They'd only view me as nosy and wouldn't tell me a thing, even though I got along well with both women.

I was in my old bedroom using the laptop. Both my mom and aunt were out shopping for a few hours, and it was the perfect time to do some research on my boss. Why I hadn't thought to do this earlier was beyond me. I pulled up anything and everything I could about him. I learned he was indeed a very successful businessman, but I already knew that tidbit of information strictly from the size of his house.

As he had told my aunt, he made the majority of his money in the stock market years before, pretty much setting him up for the rest of his life. After that, he started managing the investment needs of some of the Fortune 500 businesses, something that kept him pretty busy.

As for his personal life, there wasn't much to be found. His father was a world-renowned psychiatrist, earning many influential awards during his career. His focus was on how the human brain copes with trauma and tragedy, as well as what transformations and adaptations the mind will go through in order to continue to exist. It was a career that was cut short, however. He and his wife died in a tragic car accident eight years ago, leaving behind a daughter, Gabriella, and, of course, Mason. His father was only forty-eight at the time of the accident, his mother forty-five. I couldn't find any other information on Gabriella. It was almost as if the trail ended with their parents' deaths.

I was about to give up on my research when I came across something strange. It was an article about Mason, talking about how he was to become the next big thing in neurology. He was studying to become a doctor but dropped out in his third year of med school, right around the time everything happened with his family.

"Lila? Are you here, sweetheart?" I heard my mom shouting from the living room.

"Yeah, Mom. I'll be right there." I closed the computer and rounded the corner, finding both women sitting on the couch, going through their purchases. "What did you get while you were out?"

"Come and see." Aunt Ellie beamed. Nudging in between them, they showed me the clothes and shoes they'd purchased. I couldn't even remember the last time my mom went shopping, let alone bought anything for herself. I could tell she was having a good day. A really good day. She had some color back in her cheeks, and she could almost pass for someone who wasn't battling cancer, which brought me to another thought. Or more like a question.

"Mom," I said, turning toward her. "How are the treatments coming along? Is there any progress?"

She smiled and clutched my hand. "Actually, there is. Dr. Greene is trying out some experimental drugs on me, and so far, they seem to be working. The medication is helping to slow down the progression of the cancer. His hope is that over time, the meds will help to reduce the disease back down to something where a good round of chemo will put me in remission."

"Is everything covered by your insurance?" I asked, a little confused.

"No, but he said not to worry about the cost. It was all taken care of." She shrugged, released her hold on my hand, and stood up. "Does anyone want anything from the kitchen?" she asked as she walked out of the room.

"I'm good," I answered, inching closer to my aunt. "Is this all for real?" I asked her, as my mother busied herself pouring something to drink.

"Yeah. Isn't it great? Looks like she just might be all right." I saw the unconditional love in her eyes for her sister. We would both be beyond devastated if something happened to Lillian Stone.

"It's the best news I've heard in a long time. But how is the cost covered? Really, doesn't it sound odd to you?"

"Not at all. A lot of hospitals have grants to cover experimental treatments for patients. She probably fell under some of the guidelines. However it happened, we should be grateful and focus on her recovery." She gave me a quick hug before joining her sister.

Thinking on it a bit longer, I realized she was a thousand percent right. Who cares how the treatments are paid for, as long as she's getting better?

"So," my mom cut into my thoughts, "Ellie tells me your boss is quite the looker."

I almost choked on my water, turning toward my aunt, all while subtly trying to shoot her a death glare. She laughed before both of them flanked me on the couch, settling in to get nice and cozy. No doubt to interrogate me.

"Well?" my aunt asked. "Are you going to tell her about him, or do I have to do it?"

"I'm sure you already told her enough." My narrowed eyes did nothing to persuade her to change the subject.

"In all seriousness, honey, how is he to work for? Other than obviously being nice to look at," she added with a small smirk. My mother was not a woman who smirked, so the tiny expression threw me for a loop.

"He's fine to work for."

"Oh, that he is," Ellie butted in.

"Some of us are not ruled by our hormones, Aunt Ellie," I joked, nudging her in the shoulder.

"You can't tell me you would kick that man out of your bed if he climbed in."

"Ellie!" Mom cried out. "Don't embarrass the poor girl." Turning her full attention on me, she asked, "Are you interested in your boss? If so, does he return the interest? How old is he anyway? Is he a good man?"

She was going to ask me more questions, but I cut her off; otherwise, we would be there all day. "Mom, yes, he's hot, but no, I'm not interested in him like that. He's okay to work for. I do my job and he leaves me alone." What I failed to tell them both was that we had kissed twice so far, and the sexual tension was thick between us any time we were close enough to send each other's hearts hammering. *Yeah, I think I'll leave those details out.* "And I don't know how old he is. Maybe early thirties?" I guessed.

"Well, just be careful. You're a beautiful young woman, and I don't doubt for a second he finds you desirable. Be smart, as I know you will be."

Smart.

I *was* usually smart. But not when it came to the man I shared a roof with. When it came to him, I was as dumb as could be. I seemed to constantly be putting myself into situations that were not of a professional nature. Although, I shouldn't take all the blame. *He* was the one who made me wear that ridiculous fake maid's uniform, even if it was only for one day. *He* was the one who pulled the little stunt in his office with the freaking trash can, making me slip and fall right into his lap. *He* was the one who kissed me in the kitchen.

But *I* was the one who practically seduced him in my bedroom, after I came home from a few hours out with Eve. *I* was the one who undressed in front of him until I was completely naked, even though he started it with taking my dress off. Thankfully, he had enough good sense not to do anything, other than kiss me back, of course. But when he asked, I never let on I remembered any of it.

We eventually ended up getting off the topic of me and my boss and watched two movies before it was time for me to head back home. *Home.* It was still such a weird concept, but his house was indeed *my* house, too. Even though it was only because I was his maid. Still . . . it was the place I lay my head every night. But it was also the place that messed with me, simply because *he* messed with me. *He* messed with my thoughts and feelings. *He* messed with my emotions, and more than anything, *he* messed with my hormones.

SEVENTEEN
MASON

IT SEEMS LIKE *forever since my father left me alone in the car waiting for him. He pulled up to some sort of warehouse and told me he wouldn't be long.*

I pull out one of my medical books, flip to where I left off, and start devouring the information. I'm in my third year of med school and I'm always eager to learn as much as I can, as quickly as I can. My books never leave my side, and it's times like this I'm thankful I'm as anal with my school work as I am.

Fifteen minutes have passed since my father went inside the building, when I hear a scream. A woman's scream. I jerk upright, roll down the window, and try to listen to see if I can hear it again.

And I do.

Only this time, it's louder, filled with anguish.

I have no idea where we are, so I carefully exit the car and slowly make my way toward the entrance my father used. Pushing open the door, all I see at first is darkness, but the more my eyes adjust to the lack of light, and the farther in I venture, the more I'm able to scour my surroundings.

There are two men standing at the far end of the massive, open room, guns propped in the waistbands of their pants. They're having a heated discussion in Spanish, to which I can only decipher a few words.

They're saying something about money, women, and doctors. I really can't understand much more than that.

Suddenly, I see my father appear behind them, but he isn't alone. He's dragging a barely clothed woman, or should I say girl, with him. She isn't making any noise, but I can see she's in distress.

I inch closer, making sure to stay out of view in order to find out what the hell is going on. My father directs the girl to sit on a nearby chair, facing all three of them. Once she's seated, he circles her very slowly, muttering something to her I can't quite hear. She begins to tremble when he comes to stand in front of her.

He squats down and places his hands on her bare thighs, inching them up her body until they disappear between her legs. My heart is hammering away inside my chest. What is he doing? Who are those men? And who is this girl?

Before another thought can flitter through my confused mind, my father does something I could have never anticipated. He stands to his full height, draws his arm back, and backhands the girl across the face. The brutal force of his assault sends her flying to the floor. She doesn't lie there, though. She must have known what else was coming, because she instantly starts to scramble backward, pleading with my father not to hurt her anymore. But he isn't listening to her. Snatching her from the cold concrete, he turns her around and pushes her against the wall, his hand holding her in place by her neck, practically immobilizing her. I can hear her whimpers, but I am too shocked to do or say anything, until I see what he is about to do next.

My father is a well-respected psychiatrist. He's hardworking and dedicated. He's a faithful, loving husband and all-around great man. I've looked up to him my entire life. He's pretty much my hero, the man I strive to be one day.

Until now.

Now, the man in front of me is not my father. I don't know who that person is. He's a stranger.

He whispers something in the girl's ear, and whatever it is, it has her struggling to get away from him. But she is powerless against him. His brand of torture goes on for several minutes, until he turns her around and slams her back against the wall. My eyes fly to the two men standing nearby. Watching, they don't do or say anything to stop him. They're too intent on enjoying the show.

The girl continues to try to get away, but all it gains her is another strike from my father. The man, who has never lifted a finger to me or my mother my entire life, has struck this poor girl twice in less than five minutes. She's still whimpering when he grabs her tattered clothes and tears them from her body, leaving her stark naked for all three men to see. Four if you include me.

I can't take any more. My brain can't even fathom what is transpiring in front of me, much less give me any time to stop myself. I rush forward, and as I'm about to reach them, I'm halted when one of the men points a gun in my direction.

I know enough to stop immediately if I wish to see the light of day again.

"Dad!" I yell, loud enough to startle him back to reality. Or maybe this is his reality, a reality I never even dreamt of.

His grip on the girl loosens and he thrusts her at the man holding the gun on me. His strides toward me are heavy and quick. "Mason," he says as he draws near. "What are you doing in here? I told you to wait in the car." His voice is calm and reserved, but his eyes are telling a different story. He looks excited, his breathing coming in rapid succession. There is a desire in his pupils I don't think I've ever seen before. It's almost primal. A foreign look to me, of that I'm sure.

"What are you doing, Dad?" I'm so stunned those are the only words I can get out.

"It's not what you think, Mase. It's a clinical study I'm conducting for my new research." He takes another step toward me and reaches to grab my shoulder, but I back away before he makes contact. I don't want

him to touch me. Not this man. Not the monster I just saw.

"You hurt that girl. How could you?" I retreat a few paces, holding my hands in front of me as if I'm surrendering. And in a way, I think I am. I'm conceding to the fact my father isn't the man I always thought him to be. I'm giving up the notion he would never hurt another human being.

My entire world has changed in the span of an afternoon errand my father had to make before we went home. Home, to my oblivious life. Home, to my perfect world where my family was whole and untouchable.

Home, where my reality is now dashed forever.

"Let's get out of here, son. I'll explain everything in more detail, but we have to leave. Now." His strides put him next to me quickly. He grabs my shoulder and forces me to turn toward the exit, pushing me the entire way because my feet have become too heavy to move on my own.

He tries to tell me everything he did, and had been doing for the past two years, is all part of a new clinical study. But I don't buy it. Not one word. The look I witness in his eyes is too much of a giveaway. You don't look like that if you're merely conducting a study. And what kind of study would harm another human being?

He's trying to sell me a bill of goods, and I'm not going for it. Yes, there is a big part of me that wants to believe him, to believe what he's doing is to further the understanding of the human mind and how it copes with trauma. But a bigger part is screaming at me to follow my gut and realize my father is a sick man.

A man I now view as a stranger.

I never tell my mother about what happened that day, a decision I'd come to regret, because it could've possibly saved her life.

EIGHTEEN
LILA

THE DAYS FADED into weeks, weeks into months, and everything was going really well. My job was secure, finally, even though there was still some tension between Mason and me. We'd only kissed those two times, never to discuss the events again. He kept to himself, and I didn't pry.

He never came home with blood on his clothes again. Well, none I saw at least.

I was able to convince him to loosen up his rules some when it came to visitors and my so-called *curfew*. If I told him in advance, he was okay with my family visiting, as well as Eve. He even rescinded his rule about me having to be in the house every night by eight. I could basically come and go as I pleased, as long as I was in the house for the evening by ten during the week and midnight on the weekends, which was fine with me, because I hardly ever stayed out late. I was always so tired from my day's work I was ready to hit the sack at a reasonable hour anyway. He kept telling me it was for my own good, for my own safety. I didn't question him, because the more he talked to me, the more I wanted to rip his clothes from his body, even when he was being unreasonable. His voice did things to me. The rasp of his tone was enough to send me into instant daydreams, so the less he spoke, the better for my sanity.

One Saturday evening, as I was getting ready, I heard shouting coming from outside my bedroom. I opened the door, peered out into the hallway, and saw him pacing back and forth, his hand running aggressively through his thick strands. His temper was getting the best of him, and before he saw me spying on him, I ducked back inside my room. He yelled some more into his phone before disappearing back into his own private space, slamming the door shut behind him.

I knew enough not to get involved, so I finished putting the finishing touches on my hair, grabbed my purse, and headed for the steps. Eve had convinced me to allow her to set me up with Neil, who was a friend of a friend. I refused at first, a lot, but over time, and after I'd seen a picture of him, I agreed. He was quite handsome, and it would do me good to be around a guy my own age. I needed some sort of outlet before I went crazy. I wasn't planning on sleeping with him or anything, but some harmless flirting, and possibly some kissing, wouldn't be the end of me.

Eve had agreed to meet us both at the bar, so it wasn't as awkward between the two of us. She went on to mention that, if we were hitting it off, she'd disappear and give us some privacy.

A fierce sound startled me as I was about to turn the handle on the front door. "Where do you think you're going so late?"

I was stunned by his tone of voice, but I knew it was residual from his recent phone conversation, so I let it slide.

"I'm meeting a few friends for a quick drink." My back was still facing him. The last thing I needed to see were his fiery eyes boring into me.

"Do you think it's wise, dressed like that? Are you trying to get every guy's attention?" He was being ignorant, but I refused to allow him to ruin my night.

Looking down at my tasteful little black dress, I knew I wasn't putting any wrong signals out there for anyone. He was just being an ass. I whipped around to face him, my free-flowing hair momentarily falling into my face. I pushed back the flying tendrils and took two steps forward. With a finger pointed in his direction, I let loose. "What I do on my time, and with whom, is none of your business. So why don't you take your sour mood out on someone else." I knew I'd said I wasn't going to let him ruin my night, but my temper rose and it took everything in me to tamp it down. "Just because you got into a shouting match with whoever you were on the phone with doesn't give you the right to talk to me any sort of way you want to." I moved back toward the front door. "I didn't do anything to deserve it."

He was on me faster than I could blink. He gripped my arms and shook me, a wild look of worry on his face. "What did you hear?" His breath tickled my lips and I instantly went limp in his strong hold. "Lila!" he shouted. "What the fuck did you hear?"

"Nothing," I whispered. "I didn't hear what you were saying. Only that you were yelling at someone."

He released me and promptly went back to his pacing, drawing my nervousness to the surface yet again. Looking lost in his own world, I found the perfect opportunity to make my escape. I was almost to my car when I heard him shouting my name from the front door. I ignored him, got in my car, and took off.

THE EVENING WAS going really well. Neil was even better looking than his picture. He was tall, blond, nicely built, and had one of the best smiles I'd ever seen. He was very polite and quite funny. But why, as he was talking, did I keep picturing my overbearing ass of a boss? I had a good guy in front of me, vying for my attention, and all I could think about was *him*. It wasn't fair, but no matter how hard I tried to rid him from my thoughts, I couldn't.

Because Neil and I were getting along so well, Eve had taken off an hour into our get-together. And the time flew. In fact, it was almost eleven thirty, which meant I had to leave in the next five minutes if I even hoped to make it home on time. If I was late . . . well, I didn't want to think about what Mason would say, him already being in a pissed-off mood. Maybe he'd calmed down some, but I didn't want to risk it.

So, regretfully, I said my goodbyes, exchanged phone numbers, and let him walk me to my car. I had only nursed two drinks the entire night, so I was fully capable of driving home. When he leaned in to kiss me, I let him. There was a definite attraction, but as his lips touched mine, I pictured Mason's instead. I knew it wasn't right to do that to Neil, but he'd never know. Whatever images I conjured up in my head were for me alone. The kiss was passionate but short. I flashed him a smile before agreeing to go out with him again.

I made it home with two minutes to spare, rushing into the house like someone was chasing me. Closing and locking the door behind me, I noticed a light on in his office, but I wasn't going in there to poke the beast. Instead, I headed toward the kitchen to grab a bottle of water before turning in for the night.

I rounded the corner at the top of the steps, intent on a nice hot shower. Before I pushed the door to my bedroom open, however, I noticed the light was on. Had I left it on in my haste to leave earlier? I didn't think so, but I could've been mistaken.

My head was down, fiddling with the strap on my purse, when I finally entered my room. And because I wasn't looking where I was going, I ran directly into something. Or should I say someone. A strangled scream tore from my throat as I looked up into the face of the other occupant of the enormous home.

"What are you doing in here?" I balked as I backed up a step.

He was barefoot, wearing blue and gray pajama bottoms, and a gray T-shirt stretched nicely over his taut torso. I shook my head quickly, trying to focus on what was important: the fact my boss was in my bedroom.

"Waiting for you." He curled his lip in annoyance. "Did you have fun, Lila?" He said my name as if it was acid on his tongue.

Seriously, what is his problem?

I kicked off my shoes and tossed my purse on a nearby chair. I wanted to give off the air of indifference, acting like his icy demeanor wasn't totally freaking me out. "I had a great time, thank you very much." I grabbed some pajama shorts and a thin, blue tank top from my dresser. "If you don't mind, I'm going to take a shower then turn in."

"Washing someone off you?" he coldly asked.

"You can leave now." I wasn't going to play his games. Without waiting for him to exit my bedroom, I rushed into my bathroom and slammed the door, locking it in the process.

I was only in the shower for ten minutes before I decided I'd had enough. Frustrated with the entire situation, I wanted nothing more than to slip under my covers and fall into a nice sleep. But I guess it wasn't to be.

When I opened the door, steam billowing out behind me, I took two steps, still wrapped in my towel, and stopped short. He was still there, and it was obvious he wasn't going anywhere. The problem was I had no idea what his intentions were or why he was acting so territorial toward me.

Our eyes locked, and neither one of us uttered a single word. He was taking me in, towel and all, causing me to clutch it to my still-damp body even more. "What do you want? Why are you here?"

He was perched on the edge of my bed, but my questions spurred him to close the gap between us. Stalking my way, he stopped right in front of me, intimidating me with his sheer presence. Smelling the air around me, I was trying to decipher whether or not he was drunk, like the last time he'd approached me so intimately. But he wasn't. This was something completely different, exciting, yet a bit frightening.

"Who were you with? And tell me the truth. Don't even think about lying to me." He circled me, making me dizzy.

"I was with Eve," I said, not entirely telling him the whole truth. *Half of it counts, right?*

"Were you making out with your best friend?"

"What? Why would you ask me that?"

He stopped his predatory stalk and rested in front of me. Lifting his thumb to my mouth, he pressed it none too gently to my bottom lip. "Because your lipstick was smeared. So, if you weren't making out with Eve, who the fuck *were* you making out with?" His demeanor darkened. He was angry with me, but it was more than that.

When I glanced up into his brown eyes, I saw possession and desire dueling. He was worried about me, yet trying to distance himself. His resolve was splintering and it looked like that night was the final straw, although I hadn't done anything different. Well, except for making out with a handsome guy.

Swatting his offensive hand from my mouth, I tried to turn away, still very conscious of my delicate state of dress. Or undress, to be more specific. But my retreat was halted when he pulled me roughly into his broad chest.

"Let me go!" I shouted. "Who I was kissing earlier tonight is none of your damn business. You're my boss, not my father." I struggled in his hold, but it was of no use; he was much too strong and determined.

"It *is* my business. If you live under my roof, you will live by my rules."

"Yeah, well, there is no rule about me dating, is there?"

"There is now." His hold on my arms intensified, but he wasn't hurting me. Lightly shaking me, he continued his craziness. "You're not allowed to date anyone while in my employment. There will be no more late-night rendezvous. Do you understand me?" He shook me again when I failed to answer.

Am I dreaming? Is this real? Is he actually standing in front of me, gripping on to my nearly naked body, telling me I'm not allowed to date anyone while I work for him? That I'm essentially trapped under him and all his freaking rules if I want to continue to work here?

Is he mad?

"You can't do that!" I argued, continuing to struggle free from him. "You can't dictate my life for me. There has to be some sort of law against it."

"I make the laws in this house, and you *will* follow them."

He moved closer, his intoxicating scent messing with my head. My hormones were running rampant, although I tried to remain unaffected by him.

I was failing miserably.

Then I said something that shocked both of us.

"What am I supposed to do? You don't want me, so it's only fair to let me try to find someone who does." I gasped as the last word left my lips. My hand covered my mouth as if hiding it would take back what I'd just said.

My revelation had quite the impact on him, as well. All of a sudden, gone was his cold, hard exterior. In its place, a calm reserve took over. He looked at me like it was the first time he was seeing me. His body physically relaxed, although his hold on me was even stronger, as if he was terrified I'd escape.

"What?" He rested his forehead softly against mine.

"N-nothing," I stammered. "I don't know what I'm saying. You have me so confused."

He spoke again, completely ignoring my previous words. "I've tried and tried, Lila. I really have. It takes everything in me to walk away when you come near. When I hear your voice, whether you're talking to Norma, or someone on your phone, or even when you're singing along to your music, it drives me crazy. I've been good with keeping my distance, allowing whatever attraction this is between us to fizzle. But my resolve is weakening." He placed both hands on the sides of my face. "I can't take it for one more second. I need to taste you again." Seconds later, his mouth covered mine. And it was everything I'd dreamt about the past few months, ever since our last encounter.

I didn't resist him. I should have, but I didn't. I wanted him, and my resolve had disappeared as well. Our kiss became frenzied, and when I reached up to wrap my hands around his neck, my towel loosened and fell to the ground. I realized it as soon as I felt the cool air wrap around my naked body, but I didn't stop.

I couldn't stop.

His hands lowered from my face, one circling my waist while the other one gripped the back of my neck, holding me in place as he continued his delicious assault on my lips.

We stayed locked in our embrace for what seemed like forever, when in reality, it was only two minutes. Two minutes of unadulterated bliss. Two minutes of fantasies coming true. Two minutes to shatter my strength and throw me into a world of ecstasy.

His sexy-as-sin voice broke the silence. "I have to have you. Now," he managed to say as he walked backward toward my bed, pulling me with him every step of the way. As he hit the edge of the mattress, he turned us around so it was the back of my knees pressed against the bed. But he didn't go any further. "Do you want this, Lila? Do you want me?"

What could I say? If I was being truthful with myself, I'd been dreaming of it since the moment I'd first laid eyes on him. It was his face that filled my head when I pleasured myself. It was his image in my head when Neil had kissed me earlier.

Yes, I wanted it.

More than my next breath.

"Yes, Mr. Maxwell. I want you." I leaned up and kissed him. "I want this to happen between us. Right now."

He chuckled.

What's so damn funny?

"I think you can call me Mason. Mr. Maxwell seems . . . not quite appropriate now."

Okay, yeah. I guess it did sound funny when I used his formal name. "Mason," I purred, tugging on a fistful of his hair.

"I love when you say my name. You're going to be saying it a lot over the next few hours." He arched his brow before lowering me onto the bed. He was too busy admiring me to realize he was still completely dressed.

"Are you going to leave your clothes on?" I teased, spreading my legs and watching his hooded eyes delight with the sight of me.

When his shirt hit the floor, I couldn't help but stare at his naked chest. I'd seen it briefly before, even laid my hands on him, but it still didn't prepare me for him . . . like this. My eyes gazed over his sculpted pecks, down his washboard stomach, and to the delicious V-shape that disappeared underneath the waistband of his pants.

Just when I thought I was about to combust on the spot from the sheer sight of him, he lowered his bottoms until he was nothing but a glorious, sculpted piece of man, baring all for me to see.

"Mason?" My eyes were still locked on the amazing man in front of me. He leaned into me and smiled. "What does this mean? I mean afterward?" I was such a girl, wanting to know where we stood, but I couldn't help it. I needed to know how we'd function after this. *Will I go back to calling him Mr. Maxwell? Will I even still have my job? If he pays me, yet we continue to sleep together, is it considered prostitution? Oh my God!* My mind zipped in a million different directions, when all I should've been focused on was being with him.

He dropped to his knees in front of me, dragged me to the edge of the bed, and spread my legs wider. "What this means," he said, placing a kiss on my calf before running his tongue up the inside of my leg, "is that you'll be mine." He continued teasing me with his mouth, setting free all the pent-up sexual frustration that had been bogging me down since I'd first walked into his life, and he into my world.

Wanting to get into a better position, I propped myself up on my elbows and looked down at him. Plus, I wanted to make sure I understood him completely. Confusion would most definitely result in dire consequences, mostly to my heart. "What do you mean, I'll be yours?"

He moved closer and closer to my throbbing need, his fingers doing wonderful things to my heated flesh. "Just what I said. After I'm buried deep inside you and make you scream out my name . . . you belong to me." He glanced up to ensure there was no misunderstanding. "Only me. Do you understand, Lila? No one else. You won't be going out on any more dates with other guys. You won't allow anyone else to touch you. Only me."

His grip on my legs strengthened. The only thing I could do was nod. I wanted it. I wanted it to be only him. But, if he was it for me, was I it for him? I had to know, even though I didn't wish to ruin the moment.

"Am I it for you then?" I threw it out there. The only word that could crush me and stop us from going further would be a resounding *no.* But that wasn't the word he spoke. Thankfully.

"Yes. You're it for me. There hasn't been anyone in a very long time, because of. . . ." He drifted off, lost in his own head. I eagerly wanted him to finish, but I knew enough not to press him either.

"Speaking of which, have you done this before?"

"Slept with my boss? No, I haven't," I said, a shy smile playing on my lips.

"I would hope not. No, that's not what I meant. I meant, have you . . . ever. . . ." He didn't finish. Instead, he looked at me with his brows raised, like I was supposed to guess exactly what he was asking me.

After a few seconds, it dawned on me what he was referring to. "Are you asking me if I've ever had sex before?"

"Well, yes. I guess I am." He had the decency to at least look a little uncomfortable, even though his head was practically buried between my thighs.

"Yes, I have. With one person. An old boyfriend." He didn't look too pleased at the mention of an ex, but there wasn't anything I could do about that. It was my past and I wasn't ashamed of it, even though, if I had known what I know now, I most definitely would have saved myself for Mason. But I couldn't change anything, so there was no reason to waste any energy on it. Besides, I'm sure he'd slept with more women than he even remembers. So why was I worried about my one ex-boyfriend?

"Are you on birth control?" Talk about a switch in conversation, but a necessary one.

"No."

He looked to be disappointed. "That's a shame."

"We can always use condoms," I offered, as if the thought had never entered his mind. I started to retreat farther up the bed, but he stopped me and pulled me back toward him, a feral groan tearing free from his lips.

"I've always used condoms before, each and every time. But with you, I want something different. I want to feel you on the inside. And I want you to feel every inch of my need for you. No barrier."

Is he trying to convince me to have unprotected sex? I trusted what he told me about him being safe, but if we didn't use anything, I could get pregnant. And that was the last thing I wanted to happen. Not that I hadn't ever thought about having children, because I had. But I was much too young to be anyone's mother. Plus, I didn't even know what the hell was going on between us. It was so new and very unpredictable.

"Get out of your own head, Lila," he muttered. "We'll use condoms while your body gets used to the pill." *Well, I guess that's that.* But I didn't argue with him, because he was right. I wanted to feel him bare inside me.

His warm breath was spreading across my fiery skin, moving closer and closer to my core. His lips teased me, all the while his fingers squeezing me with anticipation. I clutched the covers, trying to steady myself for his assault. I'd only done this one other time and it was a complete disaster. I was too shy to fully enjoy it, but there was something about Mason being the one . . . down there . . . that threw me outside myself. I wanted his mouth on me in the worst way, and the only thing I could think of to hurry this along was to buck my hips up toward his face.

So I did.

And I got exactly what I wanted.

"Mason," I begged. "Please."

"What's the matter, sweetheart?" he teased. "Do you want me to lick you? Do you want me to make you come?" My eyes were closed so tight I couldn't see him, but I knew he was smiling up at me. "Look at me." His command left no room for argument. When I obliged and my eyes locked on the scene in front of me, his aggressiveness caught me off-guard, yet again. "Grab my hair, baby. I want you to fuck my face." He licked his lips, before asking, "Do you understand?"

I was so turned on the only thing I could say was "Yes."

Slowly, I lowered my hands and entangled them in his thick hair. Then I tugged. And the sound that erupted from deep in his throat almost undid me.

It was savage.

It was primal.

When I remained motionless, he reminded me of what he wanted me to do. "Lila," he warned. "You know what I want you to do."

"Yes," I panted. One simple word, yet it held all the possibilities in the world.

His tongue swiped through my folds, one long, enticing, slow lick from my entrance to the most sensitive part of me. My hips shot upward toward his mouth; all the while, my hands forced his head downward. I'd never felt so wanton before in my life. And I loved it.

"That's it," he encouraged. "I love the taste of your pussy. I can't get enough." His torture on me was the sweetest kind. With each flick of his warm tongue, he sent me spiraling toward the heavens, my body taking over and raking out as much pleasure as possible. Just when I thought he couldn't do anything more delicious to me, two of his fingers pressed inside and stretched me in a way that only added to the sweet torture.

"Mason. Oh. My. God!" I cried out, unable to hold back. I'd only orgasmed from my own doing. Never from something like this. And if the intense ache was any indication, my explosion would be the strongest one yet.

My body trembled uncontrollably the closer I was to climaxing. Mason never relented, working his fingers and tongue in succession with each other perfectly.

Then it happened.

The rush that had been building all along exploded, causing me to thrust into his mouth, gripping his hair so tight I was surely causing him some sort of pain. But I was being selfish, riding out the waves of pleasure until my body was depleted. I moaned out the end of my release, my heart pounding so hard in my chest I was positive he heard it as well.

When I finally came back down and my breathing somewhat regulated, Mason moved on top of me and covered me with his scrumptious body. His breathing had almost become as erratic as my own, because when I placed my palm over his heart, I could feel the quick beats.

"Goddammit," he growled. "That was the hottest thing I've ever seen."

For some reason, his compliment made me blush. I didn't care when his face was buried down below, my thighs squeezing against his ears so tight at the end I thought I was going to suffocate him. But talking about it . . . that was when the embarrassment appeared.

"Thank you, for taking care of me," I said a little docilely. "I've never had that happen before."

"You've never had an orgasm before?" he asked, quite confused. "I thought you said you've had sex."

"I have. But I've never had one from it." I averted my eyes from his penetrating gaze before continuing. "I've only been able to do it for myself. But it's never been so intense before." Even though I wasn't looking directly at him, I had a small smile on my lips.

Placing his hand on the side of my jaw, he moved my face back to where he could see me. "Well, I'm honored to have been the first to make you come." He leaned down and pressed his soft lips to mine, and as soon as he opened his mouth and I felt his tongue, I tasted my release. And I liked it. It was such an intimate act, one I was only too happy to share with this man. "And the last," he said, more on a whisper. I was so enraptured, I wasn't even sure I'd heard him correctly. But no matter, I was solely focused on what we were going to do next.

Our bodies were flush with one another, some of his weight being held up by his forearms. "Do you want me to . . . take care of you now?"

One corner of his mouth lifted while his brow arched in amusement. "Thanks for the offer, but I'm not wasting any more time. I need to be buried inside you, right now." He jumped off me and quickly walked out of the room. I was confused until he came back holding a condom.

My features instantly softened as he strode toward the bed. He extended his hand. "Do you want to do the honors?" There was a devious gleam in his eyes and I could tell he was enjoying my uneasiness.

"I've never . . . I wouldn't know what to do," I said shyly, averting my gaze before I really embarrassed myself.

I guess my answer wasn't good enough, because he stepped closer, reached for my hand, and pulled me to my feet. He ripped open the wrapper, took out the condom, and placed it in my palm. "I'll show you," he said, sending an unexpected jolt of desire through me. When I didn't make a move, he gripped his thickness and spoke. "Don't be shy. Pinch the tip then just slide it over me." I held my breath as my fingers made contact. A low groan rumbled from his throat when I gripped him, slowly placing the condom over the head of his beautiful cock. "Fuck," he mumbled, locking eyes with me before thrusting himself farther into my hand. I barely finished sheathing him when he pushed me back down on the bed and covered me with his body.

"Now, where were we?" he asked as his strong legs spread both of mine apart. "Oh, yeah."

His mouth lowered to mine and begged for my submission. His kiss was demanding, and all I could do was surrender to his desire.

To *our* desire.

I was more than ready, but because it'd been some time since I'd last had sex, I was thankful Mason took his time, pushing inside me slowly, his thickness stretching me to the point of discomfort.

I must've been holding my breath or making some kind of anguished face, because he stopped, and asked me, "Are you okay? Am I hurting you?" He was, but I knew once we were fully joined, the pain would dissipate. At least, I hoped it would. Either way, there was no way I wanted him to stop.

"It's been a long time, that's all." I tried to arch my back and swivel my hips, inviting him to continue, but he didn't budge.

"But am I hurting you, Lila? Tell me the truth."

"You're rather large, but I'll get used to it. Please . . . don't stop," I pleaded as my teeth grabbed onto the corner of his bottom lip. "Don't stop."

"Fuck!" he grunted. "The last thing I want to do is hurt you."

"Mason," I said, drawing his full attention, my fingers digging into his biceps. "You are a big man. Even if we'd had sex before, I would still presumably feel a bit of pain at first. But it's nothing I can't handle, and the truth is, I kind of like it," I confessed.

He wasn't quite sure what to make of what I had said. But since his need was as great as mine, he came up with something he thought would help. "Open your legs wider then wrap them around my waist. It should help."

I did as he said, and he was right. It did help.

Our mouths fused back together and our kiss became wild. He stroked my tongue with his, tasting me. Teasing me.

I felt like I was dreaming. Meandering through life, with all its ups and downs, had led me to Mason. It wasn't an ideal situation, but it was *our* situation. And I wouldn't trade one second of it for anything. Well, maybe a few seconds, mainly the ones where he'd made me wear that damn outfit.

Knowing he was hiding parts of himself from me still, maybe this was the start of him being able to open up to me. He never told me what had happened the day he came home covered in blood. I could only hope the closer we became, the more he'd learn to trust me with his secrets.

"Lila, baby, are you close?" We'd been writhing around in pleasure and I'd somehow gotten lost in my own head. "I fear I'm going to be done soon, but I'm trying to hold out until you come again." He nuzzled his head into my neck, biting softly at the sensitive skin under my lobe.

"Say it again, Mason," I purred.

"Say what? That I want you to come again?" he whispered, his tongue tracing the shell of my ear. He sent delicious shivers through my body. I was the one who was trying to hold out as long as possible, never wanting our escapade to end. I wasn't sure what was waiting for either one of us afterward.

"I'm almost there," I cried out, my body's trembles starting to take over. Then, as I was about to explode, he stopped moving. In fact, he withdrew from inside me completely. "What are you doing?" Before I could even get an answer from him, he flipped me over in one fluid motion, grabbed my hips, and lifted me until I was on all fours. Without missing a beat, he thrust back inside, pounding into me with an all-consuming animalistic need.

"Fuck, baby. Do you have any idea what you do to me?" His body punished mine, holding me responsible for his lack of control. His dominance over me was thrilling and I couldn't get enough. At that angle, I could feel him even deeper, my walls gripping his massive length until the only thing he could do was groan in pleasure. "Goddammit! Fuck! I'm gonna come, baby."

"Fuck me harder." I was at the edge and I threw all shyness to the curb. This was about pure, unadulterated need.

With one hand on my hip, holding me in place, his other hand circled my waist, slid lower, and found my clit. The pressure was perfect, instantly making me spiral out of control. And as we were both coming, he lost himself completely and marked me as his, his teeth latching onto my neck.

To say our relationship had become complicated was an understatement.

NINETEEN
MASON

WHAT THE FUCK *was I thinking?* I should have never let my emotions, primarily my jealousy, get the better of me. I had no right staking any claim on Lila. I should have kept my dick in my pants, and myself out of her bedroom. The whole time she was gone, I did nothing but pace around my goddamn house, waiting for her to come home. Picturing myself inside her was what prompted me to enter her bedroom in the first place. I never intended to do what I did. I only wanted to be in her space, to feel closer to her. But as soon as she walked into the room and I saw her smeared lipstick, I lost it.

I lost the war inside myself.

I fucked up.

Selfish.

That's what it was, and now I had to find a way out of it.

I'd hardly slept a wink, knowing I couldn't prolong the inevitable any longer. Waking very early, I left her bed. She looked so peaceful; I hated what I had to do. *I don't know what's going to happen after today.* Maybe she'd leave. But then again, every single time I'd thought she was going to disappear from my life, she surprised me by staying, giving in to whatever crazy demands I'd made just so she could keep her job.

I was an even bigger asshole than I thought.

What I put her through was inexcusable, even for me.

It was Sunday, and I was sure I wasn't going to see her for quite some time, so I locked myself away in my office, trying to get some last-minute work done. After about two hours, I was ready to shut my computer down, when my cell rang. Turning it over, I saw the number I dreaded. Ignoring the call wasn't smart, but I couldn't deal with that shit so early.

I was in the kitchen a few minutes later, but I could still hear it ringing, over and over again. I had to answer sooner or later or there would be consequences. Enough was enough. I had to find a way out of my hell, and do it soon.

Rounding my desk, I snatched the intrusive device and flipped it open.

"Hello," I growled.

There was silence, but only for a few prolonged seconds. "How many times do we have to have the same fucking conversation? You know better than to not answer your phone, Maxwell. What the fuck are you playing at?"

"I didn't hear it ringing," I lied. "Sue me."

"You wish that's all I would do to you. You need to stop fucking around. You're getting sloppy, man."

"What do you want?" My patience had run out a long time before, and the sooner I could get him off the phone the better.

"We have a special job for you."

"Fine, text me the directions."

"This is not within driving distance. Your expertise is required in Mexico. I'll send you the information." There was another silent pause before he continued speaking. "And don't keep me waiting or else you *will* regret it."

He hung up before I could respond. It took everything in

me when they wanted me local; there was no way I was going to fucking Mexico. This was bad. Real bad. I knew enough about the organization to know Mexico was where their base was located, and the more I got involved, the more danger I was in, and everyone around me.

This is exactly why I chose not to get involved with anyone.

While I was lost in my own head, my phone alerted me to the incoming information.

I didn't even bother looking at it; I wasn't going and that was all there was to it. What would they do? If I can't go, I can't go. They can't force me.

Well, they can.

But I'm willing to take the risk.

Sometime later, I was coming back from a run when I saw Lila in the driveway. She was on her way out, and we locked eyes as I passed her and headed for the front door. I knew I was being a dick for not saying anything to her, surely making her second-guess everything that happened between us the night before, but there was nothing I could do at that point.

I had to stop this before it got worse.

Not bothering to look behind me for fear I'd cave, I closed the heavy door, but not before I heard the squeal of her tires as she sped off.

My hand clutched my chest, a sudden ache starting to bloom.

Maybe I'm having a heart attack.

Maybe I'm having an attack of emotions.

Either way, I don't like it nor do I have time to deal with it.

IT WAS SIX in the evening when my phone rang again, and again I didn't answer it at first. But after the fourth time, I blew out a quick breath and answered, knowing full well I was going to regret my decision immediately.

I didn't even get a chance to say anything before he started in on me.

"You missed your flight, Maxwell. Care to explain?" Frontera's tone was eerily quiet. I was used to him barking orders at me then hanging up. But this was different.

Clearly, I was in some deep shit.

My silence was a mistake. I heard him expel a dangerous breath, but instead of him yelling and screaming, he simply said, "Fine. Have it your way."

Then the call disconnected.

I DIDN'T SEE Lila until the next day. I took off after the phone call, needing to take a long drive to clear my head. Needing to figure a way out of what I was involved in consumed me; it had been since the first time I'd laid my lips on that woman. My need for distance from her flip-flopped, but my feelings never wavered.

I was making breakfast when she came sauntering into the kitchen. She stopped suddenly in the entryway when she saw me. I turned toward her, and as soon as she caught my eye, she gave me a look of utter disgust before walking past me to grab a drink from the refrigerator.

"Good morning," I greeted, trying to remain collected, even though all I wanted to do was take her, right there on the island.

She turned my way, gave me a forced smile, and replied, "Good morning, *Mr. Maxwell*." Then she disappeared, no doubt heading off to start her morning duties.

Fuck!

This wasn't going to go well. I just knew it. But I didn't have a choice. I had to get this over with as soon as possible. If not for my sake, then for hers. I wanted to give her some time to calm down before I approached, so I finished my breakfast then went to search for her.

She was in one of the guest bedrooms dusting when I finally found her. She didn't hear me approach, because she had her earbuds in. I could hear the music from where I stood, and whatever she had on was definitely aggressive. Her hair was pulled back in a loose ponytail, and it swayed from side to side every time she moved. My eyes raked over her entire body, and I could feel myself hardening at the memories of our time together. As I was getting my fill, she turned around and jumped. She clutched her chest in surprise and ripped out her earbuds.

"What do *you* want?" she yelled. She was upset and rightfully so. I'd basically blown her off after claiming her and telling her she belonged to me.

"I need to talk to you." My tone was calm but distant. It had to be.

"I know what you're going to say, *Mr. Maxwell.*" She said my name as if she was spewing poison.

"Well, I have to say it anyway. Do you want to sit down?"

"No, I don't want to sit down. Say whatever you need to then let me get back to my job." She backed up, no doubt not wanting to be anywhere near me.

"The other night was a mistake and I think we both know it." I tried to swallow the painful distance between us, but she wasn't having any of it. The closer I went toward her, the more she backed away. Finally, the look of pain in her beautiful eyes stopped me from going any farther.

"Why?"

One simple word, yet it tore me apart.

She tried her best to remain strong, her face devoid of emotion, making it difficult for me to read her . . . until I looked into her eyes. It was there I could see the small cracks starting to splinter.

Pain and heartache hidden behind her pupils.

I hated I was the man who tore her apart, but we couldn't continue. I had to finish this right now.

"I'm your employer. That's why." I averted my gaze for a split second. "I'm sorry I took advantage of your feelings for me. I can assure you, it won't happen again."

Before I could say anything more, she surprised me by walking my way. Stopping directly in front of me, so close I could smell her intoxicating scent, she ran a hand down my chest. Slowly. Her eyes bored into mine as she spoke in a very controlled voice. "Make no mistake, Mason, I have no feelings toward you whatsoever. Not anymore. So don't you worry your pretty little head about me." Her hand continued to rest on my chest. "Can I go back to work now, or is there something else you wish to say to me?"

I was reeling. I didn't know what to say except "Yeah. Go . . . go ahead."

I wanted her to take it back, but it would've been cruel to call her out on her lie. To make her admit her feelings for me after what I said would crush her. And in turn, crush me.

TWENTY
LILA

"HONEY, WHAT'S THE matter with you?" My mom strode toward me with her arms outstretched. I went willingly, because more than anything, I needed her. I yearned for her love and comfort, especially after my heart had been torn from my chest.

All right, maybe I'm being a bit dramatic, but it's how I felt. Am I in love with Mr. Maxwell . . . Mason?

It sure feels like it.

After sharing an exquisite night of passion, he told me I belonged only to him. Then he threw me away the very next day. Obviously he regretted it, but what I couldn't understand was why. The attraction between us was strong and tangible, so what was his freaking problem?

"I'm not feeling too good, Mom." I rested my head on her shoulder while she stroked my hair. Wishing I could stay in her warm embrace forever, I relaxed my body into hers, holding on for what seemed like dear life.

Then the tears fell. One after another . . . after another. I tried to hold them back, but they came rushing forth as if they'd been chipping away at the tough barrier I tried so desperately to hold on to.

"Oh, sweetheart. Shhh. Everything will be all right. You'll see." She hugged me tighter. "It's going to all work out."

After most of my anger, sadness, and hurt had been released, I pulled away and wiped my eyes. Right then, my aunt walked through the front door, tossing her purse on the couch before disappearing into the kitchen. Pulling out a stashed bottle of wine, along with three wine glasses, she turned around and finally gave us a second look.

"Hey, what's going on?" Worry stole over her as she approached. "Lila, are you okay?" She placed the bottle and glasses on the coffee table before approaching, drawing me into a big hug as my mother had moments earlier. I was truly blessed to have two wonderful women in my life, and the realization made me cry all over again. Once I was done blubbering, for the second time, I sat between them on the sofa, readily taking the wine offered.

"Now, spill it," my mom instructed.

How was I going to start this conversation? I was sure they both knew I wasn't a virgin, but talking about sex in front of my mother wasn't something I wanted to do. Less so in front of my aunt, but still . . . the topic was going to become uncomfortable. I'd tried to call Eve a few times, but she'd never answered. I left her a message, but I really needed to get this off my chest.

So, I opened my mouth and allowed the whole, sordid story to fall from my lips.

I told them everything from the outfit he made me wear, to the new rules of his house, including my curfew, to our recent sexual encounter. After I'd spewed everything, I took a step back to dissect it all. To anyone, including the two women next to me, he sounded like a complete jackass. And he was, sort of. But there was more to him, something that drew me to him. Something even I couldn't fully explain or understand, for that matter. I knew him to be a good man at heart. I felt it. But for some reason, he constantly pushed me away.

I kept my eyes low, staring at my lap for fear of what my mom and aunt would say. I replayed the words in my head. I knew what my situation sounded like, and as much as I was angry at him, there was an inherent need to protect him. To protect his character.

When nothing but silence hung in the air, I slowly turned my head toward my mother first. The look on her face was priceless, brows furrowed and lips pursed. She wasn't done processing everything. I then turned toward Aunt Ellie, who wore a completely different expression. One of amusement.

I was caught between a torrent of emotions, not sure which tide to take.

My mother was the first to speak. "That was a lot of information to take in." She still looked pensive but continued. "Part of me wants to march over there and tell him about himself. How dare he hurt my baby girl? But I know I can't do that." She squeezed my hand. "Why don't you quit?"

"Because I can't. Besides, I can handle my job. The house is big enough so I don't have to see him regularly. What I know I'll struggle with is I thought we were going to give *us* a chance, right before he tossed that possibility out the window the very next day." I put my head in my hands, trying to shake free the daunting feeling ingraining itself inside me. "I thought he felt something for me. I guess he only wanted to get me into bed."

"That's bullshit and, deep down, you know it," my aunt chastised. "Mason has it bad, Lila. I saw it when I met him. I watched the way he looked at you, even when you weren't paying attention. Damn, I don't even think he knew he was doing it; that's how enthralled he is with you. He could've fired you a dozen times if he wanted to, but he didn't. There's something between the two of you and he knows it. In his own way, he's trying to hold on to it. Granted, he's not doing a stellar job of manning up right now, but he's a guy. They're not all that smart when it comes to affairs of the heart."

After everything my aunt had been through with her prior relationship, I was shocked she came to Mason's defense. Maybe she was on to something. I waited for her and my mom to argue opposing sides, but there was only silence.

Several moments later, my mother smiled, reached over, and grabbed both our hands. "First, as your mother, I don't appreciate some of the things that man has done to you. When I meet him, we will have words." I groaned, knowing full well the mama bear inside her was itching to make an appearance. "Second, if there is something between the two of you, you owe it to yourself to find out where it will lead. Don't let him walk all over you, honey, and don't let him dictate anything for you. But give him time to come around. He'll figure it out soon. If he doesn't, then he's an ass."

"What?" To say I was stunned was an understatement.

"I trust Ellie. If she says this man is gaga over you, then it has to be true." She winked at her sister.

"What?" I repeated.

"Are you going to keep asking *what* all night?"

"Sorry, I'm in shock is all."

Right there, in the middle of the living room, I started to slowly rebuild the shattered parts of my ego, vowing to get to the bottom of whatever craziness was inside Mason's head, concerning us.

TWENTY-ONE
MASON

A FTER LOCKING THE door to the room that held my secrets—my off-limits room—I heard someone rap loudly on the front door. No one ever stopped by unannounced. My footsteps quickened as I descended the steps and toward whoever dared to show up on my doorstep. Before I could make it there, however, Lila came out of nowhere, grabbed the handle, and swung the door open.

Another rule needed to be added to the list. *Don't open the goddamn door unless you know who's on the other side.*

When I saw him standing on the threshold of my home, I stopped dead in my tracks. He glared at me before turning his attention to feast on Lila.

Oh, shit!

This can't be happening.

We had an agreement: he was never to show up here, and I was never to disappoint them.

I broke my end of the deal.

So here we were.

"Maxwell." Frontera said my name but never took his leering eyes away from Lila. His smarmy tongue licked his lips, as if he was a starving man and she was the main course. I saw her take a step back, trying to be cautious but not intending to be rude, either. She tried to be respectful, although I wouldn't've blamed her if she turned and walked away, especially after the way I'd treated her. Little did she know, she just opened the door to the devil.

I placed my hand on Lila's and removed it from the door handle. As soon as my touch registered, she shot me a nasty look. She did it so quickly I didn't think my unwanted guest had taken notice.

But he had.

His smile became even more lecherous.

Without being invited, he took one step over the threshold and reached for Lila's hand, snatching it before she could even think to retreat.

"I'm Esteban Frontera. It's a true pleasure to meet you."

Before her lips parted to respond, I tore at their connection and stepped in front of her, blocking her from his roving eyes. Looking over my shoulder, I shot her a warning look, but instead of heeding it, it infuriated her. As if that emotion wasn't already on a low simmer. What she perceived as a look of annoyance was actually a look of protectiveness.

Toward her.

But it didn't matter. There was such an intense rift between the two of us, especially after what I'd done, that there was no way she was going to go away nice and quiet.

I should've been strong right from the start and demanded Beverly get rid of her, but I'd let my hormones get the best of me. Lila evoked something deep inside me, something I'd thought was lost. Hell, she still did.

And now look where we were—standing with one of the most evil men I'd ever had the displeasure of encountering.

When Lila remained still, I whipped around and grabbed her by the arms, squeezing to get her full attention. "Leave us." My tone was vile. There was no more time to be nice. Thankfully, she didn't argue. She took off in a huff and disappeared toward the back of the house.

She was out of earshot when Frontera spoke. "Well, she's certainly one fine piece. How much do you think we would get for her?"

Not even thinking, his words driving me mad, I slammed him against the wall. Putting pressure on his throat with my forearm, I restricted his breathing as much as I could. The scar on his right cheek twitched in surprise, his dark eyes boring into mine.

"Don't you ever fucking look at her again, you piece of shit."

Fuck! I should've never said anything. Worse still, I should've never reacted to his comment. Now he'd know for sure she meant something to me, a revelation that meant I'd just put her in extreme danger.

The very last thing I ever wanted.

I stilled in my new quest to extinguish his soulless life when I felt something dig into my side.

"You better back up, Maxwell, or not only will I kill you, I'll steal your little whore and sell her to the lowest bidder."

His words spurred my rage deeper, but I reeled it in enough to let him go, allowing him to collect himself before moving farther into my home, placing his gun back into his waistband.

The vile man walked right past me and dared to enter my office. I followed him, wanting to get his unannounced visit over with as soon as possible.

The fact he knew where I lived was one thing, but to actually show up here was another. I should've gone to Mexico. I should've realized by holding my ground I was putting more than myself in danger.

"So, what's the story with that sweet one?" He poured himself a drink and swallowed the contents in one gulp. I only housed the strong shit, so there was no doubt the liquor burned going down.

When I didn't answer, he smiled, watching my every move as I took a seat behind my desk.

I prayed my tone came across as indifference. "She's no one. No story. She's simply my maid." My jaw clenched so tight I thought I was going to shatter it.

He poured himself another drink, which only pissed me off more, then plopped his ass on the couch without an invitation. *I guess he doesn't need one, does he?*

"I know you're lying." He tipped his glass and took a slow sip, letting me stew in my wariness. When he spoke again, I knew all was not good. Not that any part of his visit was remotely considered good. "It seems she has your attention, Maxwell. And because of it, she now has mine."

I swallowed hard, the room suddenly spinning and making me dizzy, the air too thick for me to breathe. I was trapped. Even more than I was before. He had me by the balls, and we both knew it.

"What do you want from me?"

"You know what I want, what I require of all my employees."

My eyes burned in my head. "I'm not your fucking employee," I spat through clenched teeth.

"Call yourself whatever you want. Employee . . . prisoner . . . indebted. No matter to me. You will do my bidding. You will answer my calls immediately, no matter the time of day. You will go where I send you. You will do what I tell you to do, without any more issues." He stood, walked over, and placed his glass on my desk. "Because if you don't, I'll snatch that sweet little thing right from under your nose."

Before I could react, he walked out of my office, and slammed the front door on his way out. My cell dinged with an incoming message not five minutes later, telling me I had two hours to get to the private jet.

I guess I'm going to Mexico.

TWENTY-TWO
LILA

I WAS ALONE with my own torrid thoughts when he came busting into my room, without even so much as a knock on the door. "Lila, I have to go away on business for a day or so." He crossed the space and walked right into my closet, his hurried strides making me all the more nervous. When he reappeared, he had my small suitcase in his hand.

"What are you doing? I'm not going with you." I stood my ground and readied myself for an argument.

He studied me in silence, giving nothing away as to what he was thinking. "You're most certainly not going with me. But I need you to stay at your mother's until I return. I'll call you when it's safe to come back here."

Safe?

"Does this have anything to do with Esteban?" He was on me before I took another breath, his hold strong and his stare fierce.

"Don't you ever go near him, Lila." He shook me. "Do you hear me?"

"Mason, you're hurting me."

He released me right before he cursed under his breath, his hands disappearing in his hair. "Pack and go to your mother's.

Now." He departed without another word.

"LILA, COME ON. Hurry up," Aunt Ellie yelled to me from the kitchen.

"You can start the movie. I'll be right in." I had to admit, Mason's last-minute trip was probably the best thing that could've happened. I needed to be away from him to try to figure out my feelings. Plus, I really needed the time with my family. I'd missed them so much, even though I saw them most days. But there was nothing like having some girl time together, vegging out on the couch while watching movies and stuffing our faces until we passed out.

I chose *Must Love Dogs* as the starter movie, even though I'd seen it a million and one times. It was one of my favorites, and even though my mom sighed when I popped it in the DVD player, I knew it was also one of hers.

We were as cozy as could be, but five minutes into the movie, my cell rang. Thinking maybe it was Mason telling me his travel plans had been canceled and for me to come back home, I hit the side button and silenced it. After it stopped ringing, there was a text notification. With my curiosity piqued, I leaned forward and picked it up.

"Everything all right?"

I looked to my mom and nodded, turning my attention back to the screen. I wanted so badly for it to be Mason, but at the same time, I needed my space. I needed to get my head right before I even considered talking to him. Fortunately, I still had time, seeing as how the call and text were from Neil, the guy I had a date with a few nights prior.

The same night. . . .

As I started reading the text, my phone rang again. Preparing to answer, I threw off my blanket and stood.

"Do you want us to pause the movie?" My mom picked up the remote and pointed it at the television.

"No, I'm good. I'll be right back."

"Is that Mason?" My aunt leaned forward, her brows practically hitting her hairline.

I shook my head, before answering, "Hello?" I walked into the kitchen for some privacy.

"Lila? It's me, Neil."

I paced around the room, not knowing quite what to say. A twinge of guilt zipped through me, remembering I'd agreed to belong to Mason. Then anger quickly replaced the guilt. I had every right to talk to Neil, even to see him if that's why he was calling. There was definitely an attraction between us. It wasn't nearly as strong as it was with Mason, but it existed just the same.

"How are you?" I tried to appear calm, even though my crazy thoughts were driving me nuts.

"I'm good." A brief pause lingered before he continued. "I was wondering if you wanted to meet up tonight. There's a new band playing at Dalton's, and I'd love for you to hear them."

While I was content staying home and watching movies with my family, I really did need to get out. Besides, maybe some fun would help clear my head. "Sure. Sounds like fun. Can you text me the address?"

"I can come pick you up if you want."

"Thanks, but I'll just meet you there if that's okay." I hoped I hadn't offended him, but I'd only met him once and I felt more comfortable driving myself. Just in case the evening didn't turn out well.

"Sure. I'll send it right over. I'll see you soon."

I decided to change my shirt and throw on a pair of heels, applying a bit of makeup and running the curling iron through my hair. I wanted to look nice but not go overboard. As I said my goodbyes, I left Neil's number and the name of the bar on the table, walking out the door with the hope my night out would do wonders to soothe my still-wounded ego. On my way to the bar, I kept trying to convince myself to forget about Mason and let the past be the past. It could never work out between us anyway; we were too different. I was kidding myself if I thought otherwise. Neil was a great guy, from what I could tell, and it would be stupid of me not to give him a fair shot. My optimism for the night increased the closer I drove to my destination.

TWENTY-THREE
LILA

'D NEVER BEEN to Dalton's before, but I found it easily enough. The band was already into their set when I arrived, the throngs of people making it hard to spot Neil. When I finally did, I pushed through the crowd and walked toward him. With every step closer, I tried to push away all images of Mason. But they kept coming, one after the other. It was like he was destined to ruin this for me, all without even knowing it. Would he even care? The uncertainty rattled me the most. The not knowing for sure.

"I'm so happy you made it." Neil squeezed my hand before kissing my cheek. He was as attractive as I remembered him to be. He leaned on the bar and raked his hand through his slightly disheveled blond hair, staring at me rather intently. "Sorry. You're just more beautiful than I remember." A blush crept over my cheeks, the compliment something I needed to hear. "Drink?"

I nodded, pointing to his bottle of beer. "I'll have the same." He placed my order with the bartender then turned his full attention back on me, although he looked at a loss for words. So I broke the unease instead.

"The band is really good, from what I can hear so far." I shifted from foot to foot, all while trying to keep eye contact. Nerves had suddenly taken over, making me second-guess my decision to come out that evening. Maybe it was too soon.

"Yeah, they are. My buddy is the drummer." With the tip of his bottle, he pointed toward his friend, my head turning slightly in acknowledgment. When I turned back to face Neil, he'd inched closer, startling me when I realized the space between us had lessened. "Are you okay?" His brows knit together in concern. He placed his hand on my waist and I jumped.

Looking mortified at acting like some sort of loon, I apologized before excusing myself, telling him I had to use the ladies' room.

"What is wrong with you?" I asked my reflection, staring into the bathroom mirror. "He's a perfectly nice guy and you're blowing it." Chastising myself did nothing to soothe my unease. I couldn't put my finger on it, but I knew I couldn't stay. Disappointment wrapped its ugly hands around me as I walked back into the bar and toward Neil. He was busy talking with a few people when he saw me approach. I gave his friends a quick smile before I pulled him to the side. I leaned in close so he could hear me, and said, "I'm so sorry, but I have to go."

He pulled back to look at me. "Are you okay?"

"Just not feeling well." I hadn't completely lied. "But thank you for inviting me out. Maybe we can do it another time." I knew as the words fell from my mouth they were a lie. I wasn't in the right headspace to entertain Neil. Not now, maybe not ever.

"Absolutely." He smiled, placing his hand on my arm. "I'll walk you to your car."

"No, that's okay. I'll be fine." I turned away from him before he could insist, and was walking through the parking lot to my car a few minutes later.

I blew it. I had the opportunity for a fun evening with a nice guy and I freaking blew it. All because of an infuriating man who couldn't care less about me. Other than how well I cleaned his damn house. Clenching my keys in my hand, I quickened my steps when I saw my car, my anger raging through me the closer I got. When I finally reached the driver door, I jabbed the keys in the lock. Or at least I tried to before they fell to the pavement. "Of course," I muttered, bending down to retrieve them. When I stood back up, I tried again, and as I opened the car door, someone grabbed me from behind. Before I could even scream, a smelly cloth covered both my mouth and nose. I tried to struggle, to breathe, but the only thing I could do was give in to the darkness creeping in all around me.

TWENTY-FOUR
MASON

"**N**EXT TIME I call and tell you to be somewhere, you better not hesitate." Frontera's voice woke the beast inside me who wanted nothing more than to tear him limb from limb. He hung up on me, leaving me to entertain various thoughts as I walked toward the private plane, anxious to get back home. How much longer could I do this? How was I able to walk away from them every time? Was Lila ever going to forgive me? Did I want her to? My emotions had become increasingly chaotic and it seemed there was fuck all I could do about it.

I buckled my seatbelt, pulling the strap tightly across my lap. But it would be a blessing if the plane crashed; then I'd never have to deal with this shit ever again. But my luck, it wouldn't. Therefore I knew I had to get serious about finding a way out of *working* for Frontera. But his organization ran deep, law enforcement and numerous political figureheads in his pocket. I wasn't sure who I could trust to help me.

In all reality, I knew the only way out was to kill him. My survival instinct would kick in if he ever forced my hand, especially if he ever hurt someone I cared for.

Frontera threatened me on a regular basis, hinting at taking out his revenge on my last living relative: my sister, Gabriella. A woman who I rarely spoke to for fear of accidentally involving her any further. She had no idea what I was wrapped up in, and I didn't want or need her worrying about me. I wanted her to live her life as if she didn't have a target on her back.

Because she did.

Every day.

As long as I helped them, she was safe. But now there was someone else involved. Lila. I'd tried to dismiss my feelings for her, pushing her away every change I got, but she'd burned herself into me. I knew. She knew it, although I was sure she was second-guessing it, and Frontera knew it.

Lila had become my newest weakness.

Giving in to my fatigue, I closed my eyes and prepared to drift off. But images of Lila kept me awake. Remembering the way she felt beneath me. The way she tasted on my tongue. The way her body writhed when I devoured her. She was pure heaven, my sweetest torture.

I made a dire mistake when I fucked her; although, at the time, I'd meant every word I'd told her. But in the light of day, everything changed. It had to.

When I told her it'd been a mistake, she acted aloof, trying her best to put on a strong, unaffected front, but I witnessed the defeat and hurt in her eyes. It killed me. Tore at my heart. Fuck, it ripped at my soul.

I'd been gone for only two days, but it felt like forever. I knew when I arrived back home, and Lila came back from her mother's, we'd avoid each other as much as possible. But I felt better knowing she was under the same roof, safe, because I'd do everything to protect her.

When I walked through the front door of my house, I saw there were a few lights on, set on a timer for times like this when

I was away. Pulling out my cell, I called Lila to let her know I was back and she needed to return.

One ring turned into five before her voicemail clicked on. Hearing her on the other end of the phone made my chest hurt. I missed her. I wanted to see her, even if she didn't want to have anything to do with me. I hung up and dialed her number again. It rang and rang before her voicemail picked up. Again. Agitation built inside me that I couldn't get in touch with her, but I inhaled deeply before pushing the air from my lungs, willing my temper to calm. Nothing good would come from getting all riled up.

I took the time to think about how I'd handle our situation going forward. The more Lila meant to me, the more danger she was in of losing the only life she knew. And it was that simple reminder that would force me to remain emotionally distant from her, if I could ever get back in touch with her. Was she not answering my calls on purpose? Would she come back to work, or was my treatment of her the final straw to make her quit? Although that hadn't been my intention this time.

Dialing her number a few more times proved unsuccessful, so I hung up and decided to give her the night and try her again in the morning.

After downing a glass of scotch, I stood under the spray of the hot water, needing to wash away all the dirt and grime of the past couple days. It wouldn't touch the stains on my soul, but it would have to do.

I WOKE EARLY the next morning, eager to get in touch with Lila. Waiting until what I considered a reasonable hour, I dialed her cell.

Then again.

And again.

Nothing.

I started to become nervous.

Rushing to my office, I searched for the piece of paper with her mother's number on it. I found it tucked under a pile of folders on the far corner of my messy desk. Quickly connecting the call, I was relieved to hear it ringing. Thankfully, I didn't have to wait too long before she answered, but her hysterical tone was something I hadn't banked on.

"Hello?" Lillian Stone's voice only served to alarm me, the quiver instantly put me on high alert. My thoughts instantly reverted to the previous night, my failure to get in touch with Lila.

"Is Lila there?" I asked, holding my breath for her response.

"Who is this?" Her voice broke, and I knew something bad had happened. But what? It couldn't be what I was thinking. There was no reason for him to actually threaten her. I'd complied with his demands and made the trip to Mexico, doing what he'd expected of me.

"It's Mason . . . Maxwell. Lila's boss. Is she there?" Breath was a luxury reserved only for good news. The longer I held it, the more the unfolding situation wasn't real. There was a long, pregnant pause on the phone, and when I thought she'd hung up, someone else spoke.

"Mason? It's Ellie. Lila's aunt."

"Yes, I remember." I couldn't hold back any longer. Not caring if I sounded like someone who wasn't supposed to care, I spewed out my next words. "Where is she, Ellie? Why isn't she answering her phone? I need her . . . I need to talk to her. Now." I tried to rein it in, but I failed miserably.

"We don't know where she is. She went to meet Neil two nights ago and never came back." There was despair laced in every word she spoke, and I felt bad for her, but I couldn't focus on trying to console her. I needed to find Lila.

It took me a moment for her words to register. *Wait, what? Who the fuck is Neil?*

"Some guy she went out with once before, a little while ago."

Shit! I guess I asked that aloud.

Jealousy was not a good look on me. It consumed me, turned me into an even darker man. I hated the way my heart beat faster, the way my vision clouded over. My palms started to sweat and my jaw was in jeopardy of shattering if I didn't calm the fuck down right away.

Because I fell silent, her aunt felt the need to speak again. "He called her the other night to meet him at some club." She sniffled. "She hasn't come home. Oh, God, Mason. What happened to her?" She was full-on crying then.

Grinding my teeth and clenching my fist at my side, I chose my next words carefully, praying they weren't true. "Is it possible she took off with this guy?" I hated asking the question, but only because I was afraid of her response.

"She was upset over what happened between the two of you, but she'd never take off. She'd never make us worry. Never."

Choosing to ignore the reference about Lila and me, I continued to focus on the more important part of the conversation. She didn't take off because she was pissed off at me. Something bad really had happened.

"Do you have this guy's phone number? And do you remember the name of the club where she met him?" I had a hard time thinking straight, my imagination running wild.

Could it be a coincidence she went missing?

Is it tied to me in any way?

The silence was killing me. My legs were growing tired, pacing back and forth in my office. What I really wanted to do was run around town, tearing it apart until I found her, but I knew I had to remain as calm as possible so my efforts wouldn't be wasted.

"Hold on." A moment later, she rattled off his cell number and the name of the bar. Her final words were her pleading with me to find her niece.

After we hung up, I immediately dialed the number. Just when I thought his voicemail was going to kick on, someone picked up, a very groggy voice coming over the line.

"Hello?" I didn't answer at first, taking a few deep breaths so as not to scare him off too quick. Thankfully, due to my interactions with Frontera, I had plenty of recording and tracing equipment, clicking it on as soon as the asshole answered his cell. "Hello?" he repeated. "Who is this?"

"Where's Lila?" My tone was accusatory, and if he knew anything about her disappearance, I'd be able to hear it in his voice.

"Who?"

I cursed into the phone, shouting in order to fully wake him up. He sounded hungover, but I didn't have time for that shit. "Lila. The woman you went out with the other night." Heat bloomed through my body at the mere mention of their encounter. "Where is she?"

He was a little more awake now. "I have no idea. She said she didn't feel well and left soon after she got there." Instinct told me he was telling the truth.

"Did you see her drive away?"

"Uh. . . ." He trailed off.

"Did you?" I exclaimed.

"I offered to walk her out, but she told me she was okay. She left the bar alone."

Defeated, I hung up the phone and grabbed my keys, rushing out the front door with the intention of heading toward the bar she'd been at. Midway there, my phone rang. I answered without looking at the screen.

"Lila?" Hope had me wanting it to be her. Instead, a gruff

laugh penetrated my eardrum, the sound all too familiar. "Frontera."

"Is someone missing?" He laughed, the awful sound making my adrenaline kick into overdrive. The flesh of my knuckles turned white from gripping the steering wheel.

"Where is she?"

"Gone." A moment passed before he said, "I knew as soon as I saw her she was the reason you were distracted. So I removed her from the equation. No more issues."

I knew Frontera was evil, but he'd just proved how insane he was.

"Tell me where she is." I pulled off to the side of the road for fear of flipping my car. I was driving erratically, and I'd be no use to anyone if I got into an accident. My breath traveled up from my lungs but caught in my throat, the anticipation burning its way through my body. I wanted to beg him to tell me, but I knew he wouldn't offer up the information without getting something in return. So I offered him my soul. "If you give her back to me, I'll work for you full time. No questions asked. I'll be at your beck and call."

"You already are."

Pounding the steering wheel, I prayed like never before he'd agree. Otherwise, I had no idea what I'd do. She couldn't be gone. Not for good. None of it seemed real, yet it was. I clutched the phone, waiting for him to say something, but the only thing I heard was him breathing. If she was taken two nights ago, there was a good chance she was already lost. The thought twisted my insides. I needed to calm myself before my stomach turned and I retched all over the car.

"Please," I whispered, desperation overpowering my need to repetitively bargain with him. Instead of him responding, however, he hung up the phone. A string of expletives flew free, defeat splitting my heart in two.

How was I going to explain this to her aunt? Her sick mother? How could I even face them? I failed to protect her.

Pain erupted near my heart, and instead of clutching my chest, I welcomed the agony. Five minutes passed as I battled my inner turmoil, and as I prepared to pull back out onto the road, to go where I had no idea, my phone chimed. A text. An address. An instruction.

TWENTY-FIVE
LILA

'M SO COLD; *I can't stop shivering.* My muscles ached so badly I thought I'd go out of my mind if I didn't find some sort of relief. My brain told my arms to move, but my limbs never received the message. When I tried once again, I realized my arms and legs were chained to a bed, the cold steel of the restraints biting into my oversensitive flesh. I tried to scream, but the only thing that erupted from my mouth was a garbled moan.

I don't understand what's going on. Where am I? How did I get here?

The last memory I had was leaving the bar. Then the parking lot. The more alert I became, the more I remembered. Dropping the keys on the ground. Retrieving them. Turning the lock. Someone grabbing me from behind. With the last recollection, my heart kicked up a notch. Someone had shoved something over my face. Panic stole my next breath.

I needed to see where I was, but trying to pry my eyes open proved to be extremely painful, the small light from under the door too harsh. I wasn't prone to headaches, but I had a massive one splitting my head apart. I was disorientated on top of everything else. Looking for some sort of reprieve, I closed my lids. But my fear kicked back in—not that it'd ever gone away—when I heard the squeak of a door handle. A single beam of light sliced into the darkness of the room, heavy footsteps drawing closer, terror threatening to stop my heart once and for all.

I tried to feign sleep, or unconsciousness, so I wouldn't have to face what was about to happen. Miraculously, I managed to slow my breathing, but the rest of my body was a different story. I was freezing, and no amount of mind over matter would rectify my body's reaction to it.

I had no idea what to expect, my brain going into overdrive with everything I'd read over the years about abductions, real and fictional. I had to remain strong if I had any hope of getting out alive. Stoking my inner fight, I slowly opened my eyes and looked at the man approaching. No matter how much I tried to stay calm, though, my breathing increased from a slow, steady rise to a panicked inhalation of oxygen, thrusting all my reserve away with each intake. More light shone into the dark room, allowing me to see two more men enter. They were enormous, tall and broad, but I was chained to a bed, so anyone would look like a giant to me.

I turned my head toward the opposite wall, not wanting to allow them to see my vulnerability. The scene was real, no matter how much I willed it away. My circumstance unfolded before me and there wasn't a damn thing I could do to stop it. Tears leaked from my eyes and snaked down my cold cheeks. My heart hit against my chest, the sound no doubt reverberating off the four walls in which I was kept. I knew they could hear it; how could they not? My pulse beat faster, thrumming in my ears, the silence deafening. Until one of them finally spoke.

"Well, well. Look who's awake," a throaty rasp grunted. It was dark and dangerous, not from a man who meant to help me.

With my eyes remaining closed and my head still facing the wall, I heard many footsteps as intruders approached the bed. If only I was untied, at least then I might have a fighting chance.

Not much of one, but it would be something. Tied up like this, they could do anything they wanted. They could tear my clothes off and have their way with me. They could beat me, tear at my flesh with knives if they so desired. The not knowing what would happen was more torture than anything.

In all my vast readings throughout my life, I'd always remembered victims of crimes saying they forced themselves to disappear within their own mind, essentially escaping their physical circumstances so they could endure the tragedy. I soon came to find out they were all goddamn liars.

No matter what I tried, I couldn't disappear. I couldn't convince my mind to float off somewhere, freeing me into another realm. I could only feel the tremor of terror ripping through my brain, through my body.

There's no way this is happening to me. Stupid girls were abducted, girls who never paid attention to their surroundings, girls who were careless. Not me. I took care of my sick mother, for Christ's sake, took any and all jobs I could just to make sure she had the care she needed. I'd never done anything wrong in my twenty-five years on this earth. I should've lived it up more. I should've gone out and had more fun.

I was in the middle of my inner battle, when I felt a cold touch on my temple, my eyes instantly flying open in surprise. Warm breath traced the side of my face, making me jump. *"Hola, puta."* Grabbing my jaw, he turned my head to face him. "You would've fetched us a good price." He winked before releasing me. His accent was thick, but I understood every word. Why did he say would've? Was he going to let me go? Or was he going to kill me?

Forcing my eyes shut again, I tried to think of a way out, but there was nothing. No scenario that put me back into my *old* life. I heard another man approach, but still I kept my eyes closed. If I opened them, engaged them in any way, then it was all too real.

"Look at me," the second man demanded. I refused. "I said, look at me. Now!" Slowly prying my eyes open, I took him in, standing so close I could smell his cologne. I stared at his chest, because I couldn't force myself to look into his eyes. Not until he yelled at me to do so. "If you don't look me in the eye when I'm talking to you, I'm going to leave you alone with Slate here to do with as he sees fit."

I obviously didn't trust either one of them, but the sheer threat was enough to make me comply. My eyes shot up to his, and it was then I almost rejoiced.

Almost.

"I . . . I know you." My words were strangled, but I knew he understood me. "You came to the house. You're a friend of Mason's. Esteban, right?" *Oh, thank God!* There was a way out after all. I tried to extend my hand to grab onto him, but the chains prevented me from doing so. "Please! Oh, God, please, you have to help me. There has been some sort of mistake."

Leaning down, he came closer and smiled. I thought the nightmare was going to end, but then he spoke and shattered all hope.

"Lila, is it? Well, *Lila*, let me tell you something. I'm not a friend of Mason's. I'm his employer." When he saw the confused look on my face, he hit me with the rest of his words. "He works for me." He gestured up and down my body. "Doing this."

My heart exploded.

No. No. No.

It couldn't be. There was no way Mason would be involved with the likes of him. To even suggest such a thing was utterly ridiculous. Besides, he didn't look like a monster. Instead, Mason was the most handsome man I'd ever seen. And the man before me was attractive as well. His hair was cropped close to his head, reminding me of a soldier, someone trained to help and defend. The scar on his cheek didn't detract from his good looks, his full lips and deceiving smile surely enough to fool many people.

"You don't believe me?" he asked, as he took a seat on the bed next to me, running his fingers up and down my arm. "Why do you think I came to his house? We were discussing his next job."

My mind couldn't wrap around what he was telling me. He was lying. He had to be. "You're lying."

"Am I? Then how is it you're here, with me, right now? Who do you think set the whole thing up? Hmm?"

Pulling on my restraints, my body went into fight mode. But it was no use. The only thing I did was cause the chains to puncture my skin. I winced from the pain, but it was the distraction I needed.

I couldn't bear to think the man I'd been working for and living with for all those months, and had slept with, was the same man who would be involved with the trafficking of women. But the more I thought about it, the more things started to make sense. The blood on his shirt I'd witnessed, the secret locked door, the incessant need for privacy—probably afraid he'd be found out. I died a little inside knowing I was in love with a monster. Someone who thought nothing of kidnapping and selling women for sex and profit.

"Please, just let me go. I won't tell anyone. I swear." I pleaded with him, even though I doubted it would work.

"Shhh . . . hush now." His fingers circled my throat, squeezing until I stopped whimpering. When I remained quiet, he withdrew his hand and moved it down my chest, stopping to squeeze my breast. I bit my lip to distract myself, but when he tore my shirt open and exposed my breasts, I was unsuccessful with keeping quiet.

"No!" I screamed, the chains rattling while I protested, but again, it did no good. Esteban struck me. I didn't even see it coming. He backhanded me so hard my head flew to the left from the force, my cheek feeling as if it was going to explode.

"Shut up!" he said with such menace in his voice I thought the words were spoken by the devil himself. "Now, if you're a good girl and don't give me any more problems, I'll let you use the bathroom." He leaned in close, bringing his lips to the side of my neck and biting. I flinched from the sharp contact. "Do we have a deal?"

I remained still, praying he would tire of the back and forth and just go away. But he didn't. He was enjoying the complete power he had over me. I shrunk down as far into the worn mattress as I could, giving him my submission in the form of a nod.

"Good." He moved to hover over me, cocking his head while his eyes bored into my flesh. "Against my better judgment, I'm giving you back. But until then, you're my property. To do with as I see fit." So many of his words confused me, and before I could choose any of them to dissect, he pinched my nipple. Hard. "Too bad," he murmured, releasing the hardened bud before he tortured the other. I clamped my lips tighter, the cut in the corner of my mouth he'd given me when he struck me causing me pain. The bitter tang of the blood made my stomach flip.

I tried to look away again, but his hand caught my chin, forcing me to remain still. "You'll watch me." His evil smile terrified me. "You'll look at me and not make a sound, Lila." My name was foreign on his tongue, like it didn't really belong to me. "Otherwise, I'll let my buddy here make you wish you had." His hands tore at my zipper, the quickness with which he shimmied my jeans and underwear down my thighs leaving me no room for protest, even if I had decided to ignore his threat. My silence killed me from the inside out.

He leaned in close and licked at my lips, the bile in my belly threatening to erupt. "I love a shaved pussy." He forced my legs wider, his fingers splayed over my exposed skin. I thought I could fight my way through his *inspection,* until one of his fingers slid through my folds and roughly entered me.

"Please. . . ." I whimpered, wanting nothing more than the bed to open up and swallow me.

"Please what? Do you like this? Do you want me to fuck you harder?" His finger disappeared only to be replaced with two, tearing at me a little more. His hand pumped into me, and it was excruciating as he drew my pain to the surface over and over. When he was finished torturing me, he withdrew his fingers and rose from the bed. He walked to the corner of the room, said something in Spanish to the other two men, and then disappeared. One of his goons followed him, while the other, the one he called Slate, stayed behind. Once the door was closed, he crossed the room and stopped when he came to stand next to me. Withdrawing a key, he unlocked my shackles before ushering me to my feet.

"Go." He shoved me toward the bathroom, and with every step, I prayed I wouldn't fall on my face. My legs were wobbly, but my unsteady mind posed the greatest threat.

TWENTY-SIX
MASON

THE RPMS ON the dash threatened to go into the red the faster I sped toward the building at the far end of the dirt road. The address Frontera had given me was one I'd been to before. Many times. I'd always gotten in and out as quick as humanly possible, returning home to wash away the experience, a small piece of my soul circling the drain each time. The images that constantly bombarded me when I walked in on a job were etched deep into the recesses of my brain, never to be free no matter how hard I tried to block them out or drink them away. The women visited me in my nightmares, screaming and crying, reaching out for me to help them and take them away from their new lives. But I couldn't help them without risking everything. My sister's life would be extinguished if I ever tried.

I'd called Gabriella before I left, telling her it was for the best if she took a vacation, far away from her home in California. I even offered to pay for it. After some resistance, promising to tell her everything at a later date, she agreed. The next woman to pop into my head, as if she'd ever left, was Lila.

I'd fought my attraction to that woman every step of the way, but in the end, she'd stolen my heart, along with my reason, sensibility, and every fucking thing else I possessed inside me. She'd awoken my primal instinct to protect her, to keep her out of harm's way. Too bad I failed once. Never again.

THROWING THE GEAR in park, I barely shut the engine off before I raced toward the door. Fortunately the sun was still high in the sky, prohibiting an ambush. Frontera knew I was coming, so I prayed none of his men tried to stop me.

Knowing deep down I had to end my involvement with Frontera once and for all, I snatched a large hunting knife I kept at the house. I hated guns; didn't know where the feeling came from, but I abhorred them. *If you're going to end someone, have the balls to do it up close and personal.* My fist was relentless as I pounded away on the main door. My breathing increased the longer I stood outside. When I raised my arm to start all over again, the lock clicked and the door was shoved open.

A man armed with an assault rifle looked me up and down before jerking his head to the side, allowing me entrance. Four more men were inside the main room, sitting at a busted table playing cards, their weapons resting on their laps. They shouted and cheered, intensely involved with their game, not a care in the world they were housing countless women who were being sold to the lowest kind of human being. Men with no morals looking for someone to own, someone to use and abuse however they saw fit.

I wasn't a violent man by nature, even though I lived in a dark world, having dealt with Frontera for the better part of a decade. I fixed up the women they abused. I needed to make sure they looked presentable for their new *masters*. A lot of them simply had cuts and bruises, sometimes requiring a few stitches. Every once in a while, the extent of their injuries required more work—a broken arm, shattered femur. I did my best. I repaired their bodies as best

I could. It was the gouges to their souls I couldn't fix.

I tried not to make eye contact with them for fear they'd latch on to me, thinking I was there to save them from their wretched new way of life. A life they'd never escape from. It never worked. They still begged and pleaded for mercy, for me to help them, but I never did.

I learned the error of my ways the first time I ever tried. It was my first job. I didn't want to go, but they showed me a picture of my sister, up close and personal, letting me know someone was always watching her, could kill her with a simple phone call.

Their prey was all of sixteen years old. She was skinny, not being given enough to eat, only enough to survive. She had dark bags under her eyes and her face had sunken in, the harrows of her new reality wreaking havoc on both her physical and mental state. Cuts and bruises covered her legs and arms, as well as on her breasts and stomach. They told me she was to be sold in two weeks' time and it was my job to make her as presentable as possible. I didn't know what they expected me to do for her, but I brought out my salve and ointments and did the best I could.

I engaged her in conversation, asking her about herself, and at first she was resistant. It took a while for her to believe I wasn't there to hurt her. Eventually, she told me she'd been taken at a club, drugged by someone she had met a few times and believed to be a good guy. Or so she thought. She saw the error of her ways when he became aggressive toward the end of the night, forcing her to drink more and more until there was enough of the drug in her system to take her without too much of a fight.

That had been two weeks before.

As she became comfortable with me, her courage exploded. She grabbed my arm and begged me to help her. She even offered sexual favors in return. I told her there wasn't anything I could do, informing her they'd kill my sister if I went against them, but still she pleaded. It went on for about ten minutes as I applied the ointment to her cuts, but I held firm. My sister was too important for me to risk, and I knew for sure they would carry out her execution if I tried to intervene in their business.

When I attempted to leave, she grabbed onto my leg and shouted for me to take her with me. The last piece of her had broken and it made my heart shrivel with regret I couldn't be the one to save her. Her cries caught the attention of one of the guards who quickly made his way into the dank room. Without reservation, he lunged at the girl, hoisted her to her feet, and backhanded her so hard she fell to the floor. He shouted for her to shut the fuck up before he looked over at me with a scowl and ordered me to fix her lip, which he had cut open.

I realized in that moment never to engage one of the girls again. It would only bring about dire consequences for them, and for me if I wasn't careful. So I had to shut down my heart the minute I stepped in the room with them, moving about like a robot devoid of all feelings.

Essentially who I ended up becoming.

Until Lila.

I learned later on that Frontera and his men held the women for a month. Two weeks for training, which was essentially stripping them of any life they'd known, breaking not only their bodies but spirit as well. Then the next two weeks were required for healing, which was where I came in.

Thrust back into the task at hand, one of the men led me down a hall and around a corner until we came across a set of stairs. "She's in the last room on the left." He left before I could question him about her well-being.

TWENTY-SEVEN
LILA

I KNEW IT'D only been a couple days since I'd been kidnapped, but it felt like a year. Each passing hour was slower than the last, drawing out my time, all while dashing my hope of ever being rescued. I felt my old life slipping away, shuddering at the thought my nightmare was slowly turning into my reality.

Thankfully, when Esteban had left the room earlier, the only time Slate had touched me was when he unchained me, shoved me toward the toilet, and then again when he reattached my restraints. I thought for sure he was going to rape me, or at the very least beat me. But he hadn't, which only served to confuse me, not that I wasn't thankful for not being touched. He did, however, remove the rest of my clothing while I was using the bathroom, leaving me completely naked while chained up.

Lying on the smelly, worn mattress, I tried to get comfortable, but having my limbs spread and immobile, I found it impossible. So I listened instead, but I heard nothing. Wherever I was being held had to be secure. Underground even. As time passed, I grew tired, closing my eyes and praying for sleep to give me some sort of reprieve, if only for a short time.

Sometime later, the rattling of the handle, followed by the

heavy creak of the door, startled me awake. My body tensed, preparing for the worst, but whoever had walked into the room wasn't there to harm me. I sensed it. Lifting my head, I tried to see who it was, but there was still too much darkness. Then I heard his voice.

"Lila." It was Mason. At first, I was elated, but then fear quickly took over. Mason worked for that evil bastard. He was one of them. He'd set up my entire kidnapping. Was he here to gloat, to tell me what a fool I'd been to trust him? Care for him? Sleep with him? The closer he stepped, the angrier I became. "Lila." He called my name again, but still, I didn't answer. The only thing I could do was stare at him as he approached. When he stood a few feet from me, he reached out to touch me. I shrank back and he withdrew. "It's me. Mason."

"Don't touch me." Anger dripped from my words.

"It's Mason," he repeated.

"I know. Don't. Touch. Me."

"What's going on?" He leaned over me and inserted a key into the locks of my shackles. He was one of them; otherwise, why would he have a key? Reason took over, and I allowed him to free me. At least then I'd have a remote shot at escaping. I'd be naked, but modesty took a back seat to my safety.

As soon as the last chain hit the mattress, I jumped up as quickly as I could and shoved him with all my remaining strength, which wasn't much. Before I could get very far, though, he snatched my wrist and pulled me back. My legs scrambled not to trip over the other, and I smashed into his body in the process, essentially halting my escape.

TWENTY-EIGHT
MASON

A S I OPENED the door, it took a few seconds for my eyes to adjust to the darkness of the room, but when they did, I saw her lying chained to the bed. Naked.

My heart broke.

My rage built.

My breath collapsed.

I called out to her, so as not to frighten her before approaching. After the second time announcing it was me, she acknowledged she understood, but the anger in her voice confused me. There was no time to dwell on her fury, so instead, I used the key one of the men gave me and unchained her. Before I realized what was happening, she lunged off the bed and made a run for it. But I had to stop her. Even though the men wouldn't stop me, knowing I was there to take her with me, she was stark naked. I needed to both cover her up and calm her down before we left the room.

Lila continued to squirm against me. "Stop." I tried to sound forceful yet compassionate. Still, she struggled. I grabbed her shoulders and turned her around, leaning down to look into her eyes. "Lila, stop it. I'm going to take you out of here, but I need to cover you up first."

"Get away from me you . . . *liar!*" she shrieked, the sound piercing my eardrum. She kicked at my shins. "Don't you dare touch me! Ever again!" She hit me on the chest, grabbed my hair, and hit me in the face. What she didn't realize was there was nothing she could do to me that would hurt more than knowing I'd done this to her. I'd put her life in jeopardy. I failed to keep her safe.

"I'm here to take you away." It was the only thing I could say.

"It's all your fault. They took me because of you." Her words cut deep, because they were true. She turned her head to the side so I couldn't see her face. "You're one of them." Her sobs shook her small frame, spearing me right through the heart with every shake and tremor.

Still holding on to her, I pulled her into me and wrapped my arms around her. "I'm not like them. I swear. I'm here to take you home. I'll never let anything bad happen to you again." I kissed the top of her head, and eventually she stopped crying. She kept her arms at her sides the entire time, but at least she wasn't flailing them at me.

Knowing the clock was ticking, I released her and pulled my shirt over my head. Thankfully she didn't make another attempt to run from me. I placed the material over her head and it fell to just above her knees, enough to shield her skin from prying eyes.

TWENTY-NINE
LILA

FOLLOWING MASON WAS the last thing I wanted to do, but I knew I had to in order to escape. I'd deal with him as soon as he took me to safety.

"Stay right behind me, Lila, and don't run ahead."

Having no other choice, I followed his command. I couldn't escape the heat of his touch as he practically dragged me behind him, shielding my body as he tried to find his way out of this building. Wanting nothing more than to separate myself from the one man who'd actually saved me, I knew it would be useless. His sheer determination was too powerful to fight against. Besides, I was drained. Physically and emotionally.

The thing I couldn't understand was, if he'd orchestrated my abduction and worked for Esteban the whole time, why would he go against his boss and rescue me? It didn't make any sense. Unless . . . Esteban had lied. But why would he? Why would he make up such a thing?

Because he's a criminal, that's why. He lies for a living.

Trying to focus on our escape, I diligently followed Mason down each twist and turn of the dark hallways, fumbling along so I didn't fall and take both of us down. My unease was evident in each step I took.

My vision was still a tiny bit hazy, my coordination not completely on point. Taking a few deep breaths, I tugged on his arm to try and get him to slow down.

"Mason, I can't walk that fast. Slow down."

"We don't have time. We have to get out of here. If we don't. . . ." He never finished the rest of his sentence, but he did slow down. Actually, he came to a complete stop, my tiny frame slamming into the back of him and knocking him forward a step.

Leaning to the right, I peered around his looming body and squinted into the darkness. I could faintly make out someone a few feet in front of us, but I wasn't sure who it was.

"What are you doing?" I whispered, trying to remain as quiet as possible.

His only reaction was for him to grab my arm and push me completely behind him. We stood in silence for what seemed like forever, my fear coating both of us. As we were about to forge ahead, a dark and sinister voice broke through the air, swirling its evil intentions all around us.

"I changed my mind."

I knew as soon as he spoke who it was.

Esteban.

I knew very little about the man, except that he was evil incarnate. Resting my hand on Mason's back, I could feel his muscles coil. He appeared to be entering into fight mode; I just knew it.

"Get the fuck out of my way, Frontera. We're leaving, and you're not going to stop us. You're not going to change your mind. Not unless you wish to meet the end of my blade." Mason stepped closer to his opponent, daring him to try something.

"I've decided she'll be worth more to me than you. You've become more trouble than you're worth, and I've made the decision to sever our relationship from here on out . . . with the tip of *my* blade."

He continued speaking, revealing a lot more information than I think even Mason could have anticipated. But why hold back? One of them was going to die, I only prayed it was Esteban and not Mason. "You've been nothing but a pain in the ass since I met you, interrupting your father while he was introduced to his new slave. You just had to go and get involved, so you left me with no choice. I plucked you from the only life you knew, killing off your parents so the only person you had left in your pathetic world was your sister, someone you'd do anything to protect." He took a step closer, rays from a tiny window making him look possessed.

Mason's breath hitched, his body reverberating with the pure need to kill the man. I immediately felt horrible for thinking he was like Esteban.

"You messed with their car." Mason wasn't asking a question. "You caused the accident."

"Well . . . I didn't do it myself, son," he said with a devious grin. "I have people who do my lowest bidding, your parents' lives being no exception. Actually, you met the man I sanctioned for that little job." He took another step closer, tempting fate. "He gave you the key to rescue *her*." He looked past Mason and directly at me. "Did Slate fuck you like I told him to?"

Before I could retort nothing happened, Mason pushed me backward, and I hit the wall behind me. He lunged at Esteban with such force I was surprised they didn't merge as one. As he tackled him to the ground, I saw nothing but two men hell-bent on the other's destruction, rolling around and trying to best the other.

A life for a life.

But whose life would end?

THIRTY
MASON

WITH ALL THE information he'd thrown at me, I knew the time had come to end things between us. To be more accurate, it was time to end Frontera. So, in the blink of an eye and the whisper of my next breath, I unleashed all my rage and fury on the one man who had forever altered my universe.

Over the years, I'd tried to gather as much evidence as I could, taking pictures of the places they sent me, of the women they held captive and of the men who worked for him. All the information, along with my medical supplies, was littered throughout the room I faithfully kept locked in my home, a room that looked more like a crime lab than anything else. While I tried to formulate an escape plan, a way to be rid of him forever, I didn't think it would ever really come to fruition.

Not until Lila was taken.

Lunging forward, I caught him off-guard with my swiftness and sent him reeling to the ground, taking me with him, of course. I wasn't going to let him get away. I had reined in my temper in the past for fear my sister would be harmed, but no more. I had nothing to lose at this point.

Other than my life.

But I wouldn't let that happen. I had everything to live for. Lila still needed my protection, as well as my sister. After I ended the man, I had to make sure there was no more danger lurking in the shadows, ready and willing to pounce for the satisfaction of revenge.

Or worse yet . . . profit. Someone ready and able to take over for Frontera.

Pushing all the unnerving thoughts aside, I focused all my attention on the man who lay before me.

"I'm going to rip you apart!" I yelled, the veins in my neck bulging from the sheer force of my will to overpower him.

"Give it your best shot!"

We delivered blow for blow, each of our determination showing in our aggression toward the other. My lip split and my jaw ached from his fists, but I gave as good as I got. I managed to swell his right eye, as well as break two of his ribs, the bones cracking under my rage.

I was so consumed in ending the man's life I'd completely forgotten about Lila. Pushing her from my thoughts, the distraction of her image doing its best to weaken me, I laid into Frontera with the rest of my strength. Once I was able to knock him clear across the hallway, I quickly searched for my knife, squinting into the dim area while feeling around with my bloody hands. It had been sheathed in the waistband of my pants but had fallen to the ground during our vicious struggle. Having enough adrenaline coursing through me, I could have easily killed him with my bare hands, but a knife would do the job so much quicker.

Finding the thick handle lying against the corner wall, I grabbed it and attacked him, knocking him back to the floor as he was rising, ready to do the same to me. When I pushed the blade to his throat, he ceased his struggle and stared up at me, daring me with his eyes, a blank, hollow look in them as if he was already dead.

So I made his body follow suit.

Without a word, because there was simply nothing left for me to say to the man, I ended his life with a single cut, severing his jugular and carotid artery in one swipe. My infliction was precise, causing him to clutch his throat, not completely believing I had the balls to follow through.

After countless gurgling sounds, his body fell limp, a red river coating the floor with its warm, sticky substance. I stood over him and continued to watch as the majority of his blood spewed all around him, making me take a step back so his evilness didn't dare come in contact with me any more than it already had.

Since the day I'd laid eyes on Frontera, or rather since he'd laid eyes on me, I'd been cast in the shadows, an evil force slowly wrapping me in the wings of a desolate life. Struggling against the loneliness he'd forced upon me, knowing full well I could never bring anyone into my life who I truly cared about for fear he'd get his talons into them, caused me to shut off from the rest of the world. Hell, I hardly talked to Gabriella, because I feared constant contact would put her in even greater danger.

Then Beverly walked into my office one day and introduced . . . no, *shoved* Lila into my bleak existence. Even before our eyes had connected, my soul recognized hers, casting upon me her light. The light I had been missing for so many years.

But because of my life, she had been taken, something I'd tried my hardest to prevent. First by trying my very best to get her to quit and leave me alone to dwell and escape into the only hell I knew. Then when she wouldn't give up, testing me at every chance, I forced those stupid rules on her, thinking if she was safe under my roof, I could protect her.

But I didn't.

I'd led her right into the devil's den, and even though I'd

rescued her in the physical sense, how long would it take her to leave me and take away the only light that pulled me from the darkness?

THANKFULLY, WE WERE able to escape without further incident. There were a few men walking around the outside of the building, unaware their boss was dead, never to kidnap another woman and sell her into the depths of hell again.

Once we were on the road, I dialed the police anonymously and gave them the location as well as what they would find. I knew once they raided the place they'd arrest the men involved and save the women who were more than likely held inside, returning them to their families.

Not wanting to push Lila too much, I drove the whole way home in silence, allowing her some time to process everything that happened to her, in not only the time since she was taken, but the discovery of my involvement. I knew at some point I would have to tell her the entire story, but at that point, I didn't want to overwhelm her any more than she already was.

I couldn't even imagine what was running around inside her head, and right then, I didn't want to know. My hopes and dreams of us being together would assuredly be obliterated with the doubt that was most likely consuming every part of her.

THIRTY-ONE
LILA

"**P**LEASE TAKE ME home, Mason," I squeaked, my voice barely above a gentle whisper. I was still trying to sort through not only my torrid thoughts, but my feelings as well.

My feelings about what had happened over the past two days. My feelings about the man sitting next to me.

"Lila, I think we should—" he started to say, but I cut him off before he could get in another word.

"I can't be around you right now. I need to go home. I need to see my family. I need to make sure they know I'm all right." My hands clutched the hem of his T-shirt, the only piece of clothing hiding my decency. "Right after I shower and change into my own clothes," I continued. "I can't very well let them see me this way. It'll break their hearts for sure, and I can't put them through any more than they've already endured."

He was silent for a few breaths before answering. "Yes, of course. Anything you want."

I WAS LOST in the spray of the shower, the water working its magic, trying to rid me of all that had transpired, when I heard the bathroom door open. I knew without looking he was standing in the doorway. Hoping he wasn't going to try and convince me to stay, I stepped forward and cast my head under the water, the force of it causing everything to become muffled. It was my pathetic way of escaping, if only for a few precious moments.

He never spoke, instead walking back into the bedroom, no doubt waiting for me to finish up. I took my time and toweled my hair dry. I then applied some concealer to the bruises that covered the right side of my face where Esteban had struck me. I was covering them not only from my mother and aunt but for me as well. I wasn't ready to deal with the whole situation, and the less evidence there was, the longer I could remain wrapped in the sweet arms of denial.

Finally finished, I walked back into the bedroom in search of clothes. Mason sat on the edge of the bed, his head slumped down and resting in his beaten-up hands. I could see from where I was standing he was in serious pain, not only physically but emotionally. As much as I wanted to comfort him, I knew it was dangerous ground. For both of us. I needed to gain some perspective if I was going to be of any use to either one of us.

When he heard me enter, he raised his head and we studied each other, my body quivering in anticipation. Of what, I wasn't sure, but there was something there, an undeniable chemistry slinging back and forth between us.

He quickly stood and took swift strides to reach me, his hands held out to embrace me. The look in his eyes broke my heart, but I wasn't ready to deal with it right then. When I tried to move away from him, he gripped both my arms and held tight, but what came out of his mouth was the last thing I'd expected to hear.

"Lila, I have to tell you something and I want you to know I'm here for you."

Oh, God, that's the exact thing you say that causes someone to panic.
I took a deep breath in anticipation of his next words.
"What . . . what is it? What's happened? Is he not dead?" It was
the only thing that made sense.

"Who?" he asked, before quickly adding, "Frontera? He'll never take another breath of precious air. You're safe now." He stepped
closer, gently put a finger under my chin when I looked away, and
raised my head so I had no choice but to look into those beautiful
brown eyes of his. "It's your mother. She's in the hospital." I started to go limp in his hold, but he made sure to catch me. "It's not
good, baby," he continued, holding me close. His use of the word
baby was a slight infraction against the heaviness of his statement.
My thoughts instantly flooded with images of my mother, lying
in a hospital bed, weak and scared. Scared for her only daughter.

I had to put her fear to rest and do it immediately. I had to let
her know I was alive and well.

DR. GREENE SAID her cancer had spread and there weren't
any options left for us to explore. The experimental drugs he had
her on had stopped working. I really believed she would be all
right, that she would beat this and live to a ripe old age. But I was
kidding myself, hoping and praying for the best. It just wasn't to be.

When there wasn't anything more they could do for her in the
hospital, they allowed us to take her home. Courtesy of Mason,
we had a nurse come and stay with us to tend to her needs and
administer her medications. He wanted to do something for me,
and I finally relented, knowing my mother needed it. I wanted
her last days to be as comfortable as possible. I knew the end was
looming, and I finally had to face it.

Mason stopped by every other day, asking if we needed anything, always bringing groceries with him to make sure we were eating enough. Aunt Ellie would constantly tell me how he would stare after me whenever I left the room, pining for another glimpse of me before he left, but I hardly looked at him. It was too painful, and I was dealing with more than I could handle.

So he never pushed. He allowed me the time and space to continue to process everything, for which I was grateful. But I did miss him. Deeply. My heart ached every time he walked out the front door, and it was everything I could do to not crawl in bed and disappear forever.

As the days passed, I knew my mother was losing her battle. She fought the good fight, but in the end, it wasn't enough. Two weeks after she came home, I sat by her bedside and held her hand as she was slowly slipping away. I knew I'd never know another love like hers. The love of a mother is unlike any other.

It was forceful.

It was unconditional.

"Lila," she whispered, causing me to raise my head from where it rested on my arms. She took a few haggard breaths. "A piece of me died when you were taken, honey. But it was given back when Mason found you and brought you home." A single tear slipped from her eye, landing on the top of my hand entwined with hers, near her cheek. "I'll forever be grateful to him for not only rescuing you, but for making you feel something. I just wish you wouldn't fight against it so much."

"It's complicated, Mom." It was the only thing I could think to say in my defense, although I knew it wasn't much of one.

"Listen to me. You have to promise me something." She spoke so softly I almost didn't hear her.

"Anything."

"You have to give Mason a chance to make things right between the two of you." When I started to resist, she gripped my hand tighter. "He is a good man, honey. You and I both know it's true."

I couldn't argue with her, because I knew she was right. I just wasn't ready to face him and have that conversation.

My attention was back on her when she started to cough and blood filled her tissue. I called for the nurse immediately and was gently pushed aside as she tended to her patient. After a few minutes, I was instructed to let her rest. I could visit again after a little while.

Before I left, she called out to me. "Baby girl, I love you. You're my world, and although this seems like the end, it isn't, sweetheart. We'll see each other again. I promise you." She smiled and turned toward her nurse. "Can I see my sister for a few minutes before I rest?" After a little resistance, not wanting to argue, the nurse gave in and I went to get Aunt Ellie.

It was only fifteen minutes after their visit when my aunt came out into the living room, wiping the tears away as she made her way over to me. I was sitting on the couch, staring down at my folded hands.

"Lila," she said, her voice breaking as soon as she spoke. I knew from her tone my world had shattered.

I never looked up at her. I didn't want to see it written on her face. I didn't want to see it from the way her body shook in sadness. I wanted to live in my place of denial a few moments longer.

But I knew it.

I knew my mother was gone.

THIRTY-TWO
LILA

MASON HAD COME to the funeral and tried his very best to comfort me while I cried. Aunt Ellie was also grateful he was there. She needed someone else to take on the burden of my despair, trying her best to be strong for me, even though she was hurting greatly as well. Eve was standing to my left, holding my hand the entire time, whispering in my ear how my mom was in a better place, one with no pain. While I tried to hear her, to believe her, I struggled with all of it.

My mother was my rock, and I'd never see her face again, or hear her laughing at one of the many goofy movies we loved to watch. It was too much to comprehend. We'd never be able to tell each other we loved one another, and I'd never feel the warmth of her embrace after a bad day.

All she wanted for me was to be happy. She said my happiness would be my biggest gift to her. But right then, I was the saddest person in the world and I couldn't even envision what happiness would look like, let alone feel like.

I was completely useless back at the house, after the burial. I tried to be there for my aunt, but I failed. After only a half hour, I'd excused myself and escaped to my old bedroom.

"Lila, do you want some company?" Eve stood in the doorway, not sure whether she should come in or not. I loved her dearly and would forever be grateful for having her in my life, but I couldn't muster enough emotional strength to talk with anyone. Not right now.

"I can't . . . I just can't right now. I hope you understand." I closed my eyes as the tears escaped and fell down my cheeks. My body shook as I turned over on my side, not wanting to let anyone, even my best friend, see me break even more.

"It's okay, honey. I'll leave you alone for now. But please make sure to call me the instant you need anything. All right?"

"Yes," I whispered, but she heard me. She always heard me.

I awoke late into the evening. It was eerily quiet, so I knew everyone had left. Thankfully. Slowly walking down the hallway, I noticed a light on in the living room. As I got closer, I saw two people sitting on the couch. One of them was Aunt Ellie.

The other . . . was Mason.

What is he still doing here?

When I entered the room, they both looked up, Mason jumping to his feet. They had been looking at old photos, my aunt reminiscing about not only her sister but me as a child. I'd forgotten all about those albums until right then. But the pain was too fresh and I knew enough about how I was feeling to know I'd be a blubbering mess as soon as I laid eyes on them. *I won't go there right now.* Maybe sometime in the near future, when I was alone with my emotions, guarded from the rest of the world.

"I'll leave you two alone to talk." My aunt walked past, leaning in to give me a kiss and hug before she disappeared to her room.

"Goodnight." I turned my attention back to the one man who still had me all mixed up inside.

"How are you feeling?" His voice was like honey, soothing my rising emotions.

"I don't really know how to answer that question." I briefly looked away. "People usually say *fine,* but I'm so far from fine it's not even worth saying it. To be honest, I feel lost. Don't get me wrong; I love Aunt Ellie very much, but . . ." My words trailed off as I tried to regain some strength to continue. " . . . she's not my mother." I felt bad for even comparing the two, but it was the truth.

He locked his sights on me and stepped closer, gripping both my hands in his. His touch was electric, as usual, causing unrest to stir deep within. "I'm here for you. Always."

My smile was weak, but it was there. I appreciated his sentiment but wasn't sure where exactly we stood. So many nights since I'd been home, I'd stayed up late wondering about *us.* Was there even an *us* to contemplate? I still technically worked for him, since I never quit and he never let me go. He told me as soon as I brought my mother home from the hospital not to worry about the job. He wanted me to focus solely on her and what she needed. He continued to put money in my account, even though I told him it wasn't right because I wasn't doing anything to earn it. He wouldn't hear of it, though, and I stopped bringing it up.

So, not only was he still making sure our bills were paid, he went ahead and paid off all my mother's medical expenses, including the personal loans we had. I didn't know what to say or how to thank him. The last thing I needed to worry about was finances, so I would forever be grateful to Mason for the help. When I offered to pay him back every cent, he refused. He said it was a gift and if I ever attempted to pay him back, he would take it as the highest insult. To soften his words, he smiled, but then told me he was dead serious.

"Lila, we need to talk. About a lot of stuff." He was still holding onto my hands, running his thumbs over my knuckles with soothing strokes. "Can you please come by the house next week? I promise not to keep you long if you're not feeling up to it, but there are some things I need to tell you. Some things I need you to understand so you have the full story."

Tightening our hold, I leaned in and kissed his cheek. "Yes, I'll come over next Tuesday. Around six?"

He smiled. "Tuesday at six it is." He slowly let my hands drop before he moved toward the door. He turned around to see me one last time before he took his leave. "See you then."

Locking the door before heading off toward my room, a genuine smile graced my lips for the first time in weeks.

THIRTY-THREE
MASON

I WAS NERVOUSLY pacing back and forth, taking a swig of my drink every now and again while watching the clock like a madman. Why didn't I tell her I'd pick her up? That way I wouldn't be going crazy waiting for her to show up. The past week just about killed me, but I didn't want to rush her so soon after her mother passed. Time was what she needed and I controlled myself long enough to give it to her.

Glancing over at the clock again, for the hundredth time, I saw it was ten after six. She was late, and it was driving me insane. Polishing off the rest of my drink, I slammed the glass down and tried to get a hold of myself.

I was nervous and I hated it.

The last time I was that nervous was when I was called out on my first *job*. That circumstance definitely called for my stomach to be in my throat. Not this.

Not waiting for a woman to show up at my house.

But it isn't just any woman.

It's Lila.

I've grown to really feel something deep for her over these past months. Dare I even use the L word?

She consumed my every thought, both awake and in my dreams. My stomach was constantly in knots whenever she was near me. I found I forgot to breathe sometimes, too focused on memorizing her face and watching her every movement, like some kind of psycho. When we touched . . . it really was electric.

So do I love her?

Fuck yeah, I love her.

My thoughts were interrupted by the ringing of the doorbell. Walking briskly, I grabbed the handle and swung the door open with enough force to tear it from its hinges. As soon as my eyes met hers, my breathing became staggered. As usual.

She looked absolutely beautiful. Choosing to wear her hair down, her tresses flowed freely all around her. She really was a vision, and it took everything in me not to tackle her to the ground right then and ravage her.

"Hi," I managed to utter before moving aside to let her in. "You know you don't have to ring the doorbell. You can just walk in. You still have the key, don't you?"

Looking a bit nervous herself, she bit her lower lip and averted her gaze.

Damn, she's sexy.

"I don't want to be rude. This isn't my home, Mason. I wouldn't feel comfortable walking in without knocking or ringing the bell." Her eyes found mine, and we watched each other for a few seconds before briefly breaking the spell winding around us.

"Well, it *was* your home . . . before. Please consider it your home now." I didn't want to freak her out too much, even though I wanted nothing more than for her to continue staying there with me. "What I mean is, you're welcome here anytime. For as long as you like. Always."

Okay, enough of this. I need to get this conversation started to find out where we'll land at the end of it.

Motioning toward the living room, I gestured for her to take a seat on the couch. Once she was settled, I took the seat right next to her, wanting to be as close as possible for what I was about to tell her. I had planned it all out. I was going to tell her every sordid detail about my life, starting with the first time I was introduced into that world of wickedness.

But first, I needed another escape. "Can I get you something to drink?"

"Sure," she answered, already fidgeting with the hem of her skirt. "I'll have some water."

"Be right back." I rushed into the kitchen, grabbed her drink, and made my way back toward her, toward a night that would hopefully change our relationship.

For the better.

Knowing she'd been through hell the past few weeks, I was trying to remind myself to go slow, take my time explaining everything. My natural instinct was to distance myself and shut down, but I knew I couldn't do that. I had to remain open. Open to the possibilities of what the night could bring, for both of us.

It'd been so long since I opened up to another person, pouring out all my fears and insecurities, essentially exposing the most vulnerable parts of myself. It had to be done, though. Not only did I want Lila to fully understand I had no choice in what I'd been involved with, but I was sick and fucking tired of carrying around the burden.

The soul-crushing secret.

Once I took my seat, I made sure to keep some distance between us, both emotionally as well as physically. I was about to be more open than I'd ever been in my life, but my guard was still raised, knowing I still required some kind of protection for what was about to fall from my lips.

I took a deep breath, held her gaze, and started. "I need to tell you why I was involved with Frontera." His name was like poison on my tongue.

She moved her body on the cushion so she was closer to me, her leg touching mine. "I guessed from what he said you were forced into doing whatever you did for him." Her brows furrowed, a confusing thought running through her inquisitive mind. "What *did* you do for him?"

"I fixed the girls he held captive." It felt strange to say those words aloud, and when she moved back, I knew how much of an impact they'd actually had.

"What?" Her voice rose an octave. "What exactly does that mean?"

"Exactly what I said." My tone was a bit curter than I intended. Old habit of rushing into defense mode. I calmed myself enough to continue with my hellish story. "After they abducted the girls, they'd begin a process called breaking. They'd strip them of their pasts, a lot of times doing it with drugs that would also make the girls more compliant. But the stronger ones, the ones who had a harder time letting go and accepting their new fate, were punished. They would do anything from slapping them around to actually breaking their bones. Rape was a big form of punishment as well, essentially breaking their spirits." I blew out a breath. "I was brought in to fix their physical state."

By that time, she was standing then pacing back and forth. "But why would they pick you to do this? How did you get involved with them?" She halted her movements and glared at me, her body shaking a bit in her sudden anger. "What did you *do* that caused you to get in bed with the likes of *that* man?"

Jumping to my feet, I held up my hands in surrender, trying to calm her down before it all went south, and fast. "I didn't do a fucking thing but be related to a sick man. A man who threw me into *his* world, kicking and screaming."

"What do you mean?"

"Can we please sit back down? You're making me nervous."
I attempted a smile, but it faltered. She stopped pacing and took
her seat. I did the same.

"Can you start from the beginning?"

"Sorry. Sure." I reached for my glass and drained the few drops
that were left. "Eight years ago my father basically forced me into
this life." When I saw she wanted to interrupt, I held up my hand
and she knew I needed to get it all out before she asked any more
questions.

"I guess I should start by telling you my father was a world-renowned psychiatrist. The study he was conducting was how the
brain deals with trauma, or some shit like that. One day, he told
me he had to make a stop and for me to wait in the car until he
came back out. Thinking back on it now, I think he wanted me to
know what he was up to. I think he wanted to confide in me, maybe
even get me involved in the same way he was. To have someone
else share in his depravity. Of course, he played it off as research,
being the true coward he was and not admitting the truth . . . that
he was a sick fucking man."

I saw the look of utter confusion on her face, and I was puz-
zled at first. Then I reflected on my words, and I knew I really
hadn't explained it too well, spewing out the words as fast as my
memory would allow. I had to slow down if she was going to fully
understand.

"On that day, as I was waiting for my father in the car, I heard
a woman's scream. I knew something was wrong so I went to
check things out. I could never have imagined what I walked into."
I paused, trying to gain the strength to go back there again. "I saw
him abuse a young girl, striking her as if she meant nothing. In
their world, I guess she didn't. I truly believe he was going to rape
her had I not interrupted him. He tried to play the whole scene

off as research he was doing, that it was for the good of mankind or some bullshit. But I saw right through him. Our relationship changed in the blink of an eye, and the man I knew my whole life died that day."

I rose from the couch again, doing some of my own pacing. I couldn't sit still for the next part, my heart already hammering away in my chest. "I found out later my father's new obsession was costing him a lot of money, buying as many women as he could, disposing of them when he was finished with his *research*. He owed Frontera big, and when he couldn't pay up, he threatened to go to the police, to tell them everything about the organization and what they were doing. In retrospect, I think my father was going mad, which was ironic, since he was the one who was supposed to be an expert of the mind. Anyway, Frontera decided he'd had enough, and as you heard him confess to both of us, he had both him and my mother killed by rigging their car. I'd always thought it was foul play, but I could never prove it. Not until he admitted it."

I poured myself another drink, needing the crutch to finish the story once and for all. "The only family I had left was my sister, Gabriella. She's three years my junior and I'd do anything to protect her, which was no secret. You see, Frontera found out I was in medical school, a prodigy in my field, so when he saw his opportunity, he took it. He blackmailed me into helping him, threatening the life of my sister if I didn't comply. I saw what he was capable of, what my father was involved in, and I knew he wasn't bluffing. So I quit school and went to work for him instead."

I took a minute's rest, allowing her time to speak if she so desired.

"You told Aunt Ellie you made your money in the stock market and managed investment portfolios. Is that true? Or was it just a lie?" She sounded hurt, but I couldn't tell by what.

"No, it was all true. I did make the majority of my money

playing the stock market, taking most of my inheritance from my parents' passing and investing it wisely. And I do currently manage several portfolios. The money Frontera paid me to work for him is still sitting in an account. I've never touched it, and I never will. Blood money has a way of coming back on you, and I don't want any part of that shit."

At that point, she seemed satisfied with what I'd revealed. There were some things, however, which I was never going to dredge back up, memories so bad I still had nightmares.

I shortened the distance between us and took my seat next to her once more. Grabbing her hand, I pulled her close. When I could feel the warmth from her body, my nerves calmed. "Is there anything else you want to ask me?"

She shook her head. "No."

We sat in silence for several minutes, both of us thinking of what to say or do next. When it became too much, I broke the uneasiness. "Lila," I said, still holding onto her hand. "I'm not sure where we go from here, but I'd love to try to forge ahead, with you, if you'll have me."

Her eyes welled before her tears spilled over, her emotions too much to contain. I wasn't sure if it was a good sign or not. She could be happy I wanted something more between us, or she could be upset because she didn't know how to tell me she didn't want the same thing I did.

Deciding to pull the trigger, I blurted the words I'd never said to anyone other than my family. "I love you," I practically shouted, my voice wrapping around her like a shield. I made the decision to lay my heart out there for her before she could say anything that would make me change my mind. *She may not feel the same way about me, but dammit, I have to get this out before it eats me up from the inside.* "I figured I'd be alone for the rest of my life, never to feel for a woman the way a man is supposed to. But then, you were shoved into my life." I smirked, trying to lessen the overly serious moment. It worked. There was a tiny smile on her lips as she continued to watch me, her breathing accelerating the more I spoke. "I did and said things I will regret for all my days, but please know my heart won't beat without you. I can't breathe if you're not with me. My soul will shatter if your warmth is taken away."

She pulled her hands from mine and backed up, looking as if she was about to utter something that would be the death of me.

Please don't destroy my world and tell me you don't feel the same.

THIRTY-FOUR
LILA

'D WAITED WHAT seemed like forever for him to speak those words to me. Many a night, my hopes would keep me awake, restless to succumb to the dream I would surely have of him. I knew, or at least I thought, there was no way he'd ever really want to be with me. My heart was crushed when he *changed his mind* after the night we had come together.

But now, he's handing me his greatest gift.

His heart.

But will he take it back again if he gets scared?

Wiping the rest of the tears away, I stood up and walked toward the window. I needed time to get my bearings. Wanting nothing more than to throw myself into his arms and profess my love, I had to rein in my array of emotions and proceed with caution. My mom had always told me never to show my cards, to not let any man be privy to exactly how I was feeling, because they'd only serve to use it to their benefit. She tried to instill the vital thought that the man should chase the woman and not the other way around. And while she was only going off her experience with my father, I didn't totally disagree with her way of thinking. Letting a man know how much you cared for him certainly put you in the vulnerable position, and who wanted to be that person? Although, she had wanted me to allow Mason the chance to fix things between us. And besides, he just expressed his feelings and put himself out there.

Does it mean he's the vulnerable one now?

"Are you okay?" he asked as he inched closer. I could feel him behind me; my body knew when he was close, even when I couldn't see him. Battling my feelings was certainly draining, and in the end, I knew my heart was going to win over my head.

So why even fight it?

Slowly turning to face him, I took the first step toward the rest of my life. Putting one foot in front of the other, I crushed the distance between us until I was directly in front of him, so close I actually had to look up to see his face. His warm breath fanned my face, his very essence holding me still.

They say the eyes are the windows to the soul, but I hadn't believed that saying until that very moment. Looking into his beautiful browns, I knew the words he'd spoken he felt with every fiber of his wonderful being. He'd put himself out there, exposing the most susceptible part of himself. I could see the silent agony written all over his face.

I had to put him out of his misery.

I had to let him know I felt the same way.

Rising up on my tiptoes, I wrapped my arms around his neck and drew him closer, gliding my mouth over his as I said the words that would set me free.

"I love you, too, Mason. I've been in love with you for some time, but I didn't want to be." When he looked at me in confusion, I spoke again to clarify. "You weren't the nicest person to me—" I said as he cut me off.

"I'm so sorry. I didn't mean—"

It was my turn to cut him off. I closed my mouth over his

again, accomplishing what I'd set out to do: get him to stop talking. I knew he felt bad about everything, and we could discuss that later, but right then, I needed to tell him how I felt.

"I need to get this all out, so let me say what I have to."

"Okay."

"I now know you were trying to distance yourself from me right from the beginning, doing your best to protect me from what you were involved in. But I didn't know it then. I couldn't understand why you'd avoid me at all costs, leaving the room as soon as I walked in. Then you'd turn around and give me a hard time when I went out with friends, acting every part the jealous boyfriend. The couple of times we actually gave in to our desires were both a blessing and a curse. The chemistry between us was intense, but you'd retreat afterward, making me second-guess myself.

"While your treatment toward me was always confusing, I knew you felt something for me. At first, I thought it was purely lust, but then when I caught you watching me every now and then, I knew it was more than that. I brushed off all your crazy antics as best I could, but they still affected me. *You* affected me."

I was thrilled he allowed me to get it all off my chest, although I knew him enough to know it was killing him to remain silent. So I quickly tried to finish up. "Then when you were there for me when my mom died, I knew I wasn't just someone who meant nothing to you. Never mind you rescued me and saved my life."

My brow arched and I tried to make light of the situation, but the reality of it was he did truly save me, in more ways than one. For the past couple years, my mother had been my sole focus, foregoing dating and most friendships. I just didn't have the time. Between work, caring for her, and the occasional nights out with Eve, I'd been slowly losing myself. I wouldn't change a second of it, though, because it'd brought me to him, the man I was destined to be with all along.

Suddenly, my exhaustion took hold, rendering me practically useless. I took a breath and broke the brief connection between us, moving back.

"Don't pull away from me," he said as he drew me close again, his meaning all-encompassing.

After everything I'd been through, his words sliced right through to the heart of me, righting every wrong that had been done. "Never again," I whispered.

His voice was raspy the next time he spoke. "I think we should go upstairs." He quirked his brow at me. "Don't you?" He licked his lips and grabbed my hand, pulling me behind him, not waiting for my answer. Then again, he knew what it was going to be.

Once inside his bedroom, we didn't waste any time, both of us knowing full well life was way too short. "Is there anything you want me to do?" I asked as I unbuttoned his shirt, letting my fingers linger over the skin of his toned chest. His body was on fire and I wanted nothing more than to be the one to quench that burn for him.

"Your touch is enough for me, baby." He smiled his sexy grin, making my movements quicken in my haste to get rid of his clothing. A low rumble started in his chest, and when it erupted from his mouth, I knew I was in for it. I had no idea what was so funny, but I knew it was going to throw me for a loop, pretty much like everything he had done or said recently.

"Actually, I *do* know what you can do."

"Anything," I said, my words uttered on a whisper.

"You could wear that sexy fucking maid's uniform." The look of annoyance on my face halted his laughter. "Too soon?"

"Yeah . . . too soon," I answered, a small smile finding its way onto my lips.

There was something to be said about being in love with the one you were giving yourself to, mind, body, and soul. Every touch was like heaven, making my skin crave his attention.

Although our passion was crazy intense, we decided to take things nice and slow. Last time was wonderful, but it was frenzied, because neither one of us could help it—not that I was complaining. To be enraptured by pure lust was something wonderful, but what we had in that moment was even better. We were going to take our time and savor one another.

Once we had both shed all our clothing, he positioned me on top of his bed, hovering over me as if he was guarding me. His warm lips trailed my body, starting with my mouth and eventually making his way down toward the one place that yearned for his warmth. Kissing my inner thigh, his slight stubble both rough and welcome, he did a great job of readying my body for his assault. When he lightly bit the sensitive flesh, I arched my back and grabbed onto his shoulders, steadying myself for what was about to happen.

"Do you like when I do this?" he asked, his tongue lapping at the affected area. "Do you like it when I bite you? Do you want me to do it again?" Not waiting for my verbal answer, because my body was doing my bidding, he bit down again, a little rougher that time. The pressure caused me to gasp, a feeling of euphoria floating around me as if it might be the missing piece.

I would have never thought that kind of foreplay was such a turn-on, but my body reacted in ways I'd never expected. His teeth grating over my delicate flesh was something out of this world. He knew exactly how much pressure to use, never breaking the skin. Then his tongue would sweep over the area, quickly soothing away any residual pain. The contrast was almost too much to bear, but it drove me toward heights I'd never known existed.

"I love teasing you," he groaned, his lips finally wrapping around my clit, baring his teeth and biting down ever so gently. The contrast between his bite and his warm tongue caused my body to convulse, tremors shooting through me and pushing me toward my release.

His need for me was beyond animalistic. It was like he was claiming me for life, the way he wove himself deep into the fibers of my existence. "Mason," I cried out, the pleasure within me built beyond my control. I writhed under his mouth, short, choppy breaths escaping my lips as I screamed his name before falling into the wonderful abyss of my climax.

He worshipped me with his mouth until I finally came back down from his extraordinary torture. Moving up the bed, he found my lips with his and bit down gently before devouring me. Lining himself up, he pushed every glorious, thick inch inside me, hitting every sensitive nerve along the way. My muscles clutched him, squeezing then stretching to allow him to fill me completely. Taking his time, he teased me unmercifully, driving me slowly out of my mind with my need for him.

"Fuck, Lila," he grunted. "I could live inside you." I smiled, but it quickly faltered as he increased his tempo. Clutching at his back, I met his every thrust until we both succumbed to the thrill of our joining.

It took us both a few minutes to come back down, and it was then I noticed the weight of his body slowly becoming too much for me to breathe. When I tried to move, making a small grunting noise, he chuckled and pushed his weight off me. "Sorry."

"You can smother me anytime." I laughed as I ran my hands through his hair, parts of it sticking up from the sweat of his exertion.

He had never looked sexier.

"I plan to not only smother you, but devour every inch of you. Inside and out." He made his way to the edge of the bed, grabbing my hand and pulling me behind him.

As we walked toward the bathroom, I asked him something

that coincidentally caused a slight blush to steal across my entire body. "Mason?"

Never looking back, he answered, "Yeah?"

"When are you going to let me pleasure you? You know . . . in that way?" My strides quickened the closer we got to the door.

"Funny you should ask." His grip on my hand tightened with excitement. He closed the bathroom door behind us and flipped the shower on, letting the hot water steam up the mirrors. Once he deemed the temperature just right, he directed us into the stall and under the spray. "You can *pleasure* me now, sweetheart. That is, if you want to." He looked pensive until he saw pure desire written across my face, the glint in my eye telling him how much I wanted to taste him.

So right there, in the heat of not only the water but the love we had for one another, I sank to my knees and took him into the warmth of my mouth, pleasuring him in ways that made him squirm in my hold. Before he lost control, he took me again, making love to me against the shower wall and draping me in ecstasy.

In his love and security.

In his passion and dominance.

As our bodies were wrapped around each other, I knew we'd always be connected, not only in our hearts but in our souls. It was hard to explain, but both of us felt it, knew it deep down as if it had been ingrained inside us since we were created. It took our circumstances for us to finally come together, to find each other after a lifetime separated by daily living and existence.

THIRTY-FIVE
MASON

S INCE WE'D DECIDED to take our relationship to the next level and *forge ahead*, as I so gracefully put it, I couldn't have been happier. It was like a light went on inside us both, but mainly in myself. My world was brighter and there was a spring in my step. I never stopped smiling, and the sight was pure heaven not only to me, but also to Lila. My happiness had a peaceful effect on her, calming her when she became anxious, since she was still a little jumpy over the slightest noise. My demeanor toward life had changed, talking constantly about making a difference in the world. I still carried around a huge weight because of what I was forced to do all those years. Lila constantly reminded me I didn't have a choice, that anyone else in my shoes would have done the same exact thing. It was still difficult to deal with, but with her by my side, I was adjusting and moving on.

I decided the best way to move ahead and try to right the wrong of the whole situation was to start a charity and use all the money Frontera had paid me to fund it. I needed to help as many victims as I could, even though I knew it wouldn't change the past or save the women who I didn't help . . . couldn't help.

Telling Lila about my plan caused her to squeal in excitement.

Since she was definitely on board, I decided to hire her to help me run it, since she couldn't very well continue being my maid. I had taken on someone else for the position, an older, portly woman who obtained her own residence.

Discussing all the details with her, I realized I eventually wanted to expand my vision and create safe houses for domestic violence victims, as well as places to teach self-defense classes. I wanted to do my part to help end the horror of human trafficking, and what better way to do so than using the very same money that came from that hell?

ONE NIGHT, A couple months after everything had settled down, I told Lila my sister was coming for a visit. I'd been in contact with her almost daily since everything with Frontera had ended. Finally filling her in on everything, she was understandably upset, but not because she'd had a target on her back. No, she was angry with me, because I'd kept it from her. She wanted to be there for me and help me, but she couldn't. No one could help me. I had to figure it out on my own and end things myself. I refused to deliberately involve anyone, which was why I'd remained alone for so long.

"When is she going to be here?" Lila nervously paced around the bedroom. She didn't even allow me to answer before she threw out another question. "What if she doesn't like me?" She was doing quite the job on her lip, biting it then releasing, repeating the process until approached. Leaning in, I pulled her lip from her teeth and placed a calming kiss on her mouth. "Calm down, baby. Gabriella will love you. Don't worry so much."

"It's just . . . she's the only family you have, and I want everything to go perfect." With her red mane swirling all around her, she scampered off into the walk-in closet to grab a nightshirt.

Lila had moved in with me again close to a month after her mother passed away. Her aunt got her own place, deciding not to stay in the apartment she'd briefly shared with Lila and her sister. I offered to let her stay with us, seeing as how the house was huge, but she refused, wanting to give us our privacy.

I really liked her, and I was happy she and Lila had such a close relationship. I could relate, since my sister and I were becoming closer as each day passed. She was married with a child on the way. Her husband wouldn't be able to make the trip with her, but I had met him briefly during one of our Skype calls. She seemed really happy, but just in case, I threw out the older brother warning to him, making him a little nervous. But he smiled and said he'd cut off his arm before he'd hurt her. A little dramatic, but I totally understood, feeling the same toward Lila.

When we retired for the evening, I wrapped my leg over hers, snuggling her into me to calm my beating heart. I hated nighttime. I was still plagued with nightmares, but they lessened each night, and I believed it was solely because of the woman trapped next to me.

I was sure I was a pain, constricting her movements, but she never complained, understanding my need for her closeness.

Little did she know I intended to keep her close to me for the rest of our lives. I had something in the works, and God willing, she'd promise to be mine forever in a few short days.

THIRTY-SIX
MASON

TAKING ONE LAST look in the car mirror, making sure my tie wasn't crooked, I noticed Lila running her hands over the tops of her thighs, rumpling her black dress. I convinced her we needed to get dressed up and go out for a nice evening. We almost didn't make it, though. The look she gave me back at the house when she saw me in my suit almost made me toss her on the bed, her new dress be damned. "Stop fidgeting, honey. You look fantastic." Her nerves heightened mine, but I tried to remain calm. I was already on edge, hoping and praying everything went according to plan that evening.

"I can't stop. I'm so nervous." Her hands ran through her glorious hair for the hundredth time.

Once we were in front of the restaurant, I wrapped her in my embrace and tried to calm her down. "Everything will be fine. Trust me." Leaning down to secure my promise, I kissed her lips with a sweetness I knew she needed. I could've easily ravaged her, but I didn't need her walking into the restaurant looking truly flushed. She would've felt even more exposed, and I couldn't have that.

The hostess led us to our reserved, private section. The space was quaint yet elegant, and I smiled big, because it was perfect. As we were about to take our seats, it was then my *guests* came into view, surprising the lovely woman walking by my side. Looking to her friends and aunt then back to me, she gasped. But there was a look of confusion plastered on her beautiful face. "I don't understand" was all she muttered, trying her best to regain some of her composure.

"Mason invited us all to dinner," Beverly said, rising from her seat to come closer. They hadn't seen each other in a little while, and Lila was excited to spend some time with the old woman. I'd forever have a place in my heart reserved for Beverly. She was like a second mother to me, caring for me when I'd given up on myself. She didn't know what I was involved in while she worked for me, but she was smart enough to know it was dark and secretive. She'd never pried though, instead doing her job, all the while looking after me.

I was thrilled Ellie, Eve, and Gabriella were also able to make it. I needed all the people who were important in our lives to witness what I had planned. I saw when Lila's eyes connected with Gabriella, her hands starting to fidget again, toying with the hem of her dress. My fingers squeezed her side, my attempt to calm her, but it wasn't working.

"Gabriella," I called out, "this is Lila. Lila, this is my baby sister, Gabriella."

"Please stop referring to me as your baby sister." She laughed as she rounded the table, pulling me in for a big hug. Anyone with eyes could see we were related. Not only did we have the exact same hair color, which was a dark chestnut, but our brown eyes had the same hue, a slight amber effect around the iris. While my hair was short, a slight wave to the texture, hers was much longer, falling just below her shoulder blades. Her pert nose was the biggest difference between us, thankfully. I couldn't imagine my masculine nose on her face.

Once she released me, she stepped toward Lila and drew her into a hug. Looking back over at me, she said, "I'm only two and a half years younger than you."

"Three," I quipped.

Ignoring me, she focused back on my woman. "Lila, it's a true pleasure to meet you. My brother has told me so much about you. And even though he seems indestructible, I have to warn you to be careful with him. He's still a fragile little boy." She was teasing me, and my laughter gave away the fact I knew it. Anyone could see the love between us was strong, and I was beyond thrilled she was back in my life. I'd been such a loner, fearing I'd sink into a world of depression, not really connecting with anyone—except Lila, of course. But a man needed his family and friends in his life to feel somewhat complete.

In passing conversations with Lila, I'd mentioned a group of guys I used to hang out with, our friendship springing from grade school and continuing on to college. But when I was forced to work for Frontera, I cut all ties, not wanting to drag them down with me. *Now, all I have to do is reconnect with them.*

Noticing everyone chatting amongst themselves, I pulled Gabriella aside to go to the bar with me. Once we were out of earshot, I dove right in. "So, what do you think, sis? Is she a keeper or what?" I questioned, leaning up against the lip of the bar, waiting for the bartender to return with our order.

She bumped her shoulder to mine, smiling wide. "I like her already, Mason. And the way she looks at you . . . you must have put a spell on her." She laughed and turned to pick up two of the three drinks.

"No spell, I assure you. It's simply my natural charm." I thought I heard her mumble "oh boy" as I walked back toward the table, but I wasn't quite sure.

We were an hour into our evening when I stood and faced the

table. The suit I wore was driving me a little crazy. I wasn't used to being confined to the fine fabric, but I wanted the night to be special, so I made sure to look the part.

Lila looked up at me, a tendril of hair falling over her eye before she gently swiped it away. When I started to speak, she knew something was up. She quickly averted her eyes from mine and looked for comfort in those of both her aunt Ellie and her best friend Eve. Gabriella reached across the table and squeezed Lila's hand, taking her off-guard for a split second. My sister knew what I was about to do, because I'd spoken with her a few days before.

Looking at everyone who had come, I started my little speech, my heart beating so fast I figured they could all hear it. "Thank you to each and every one of you who has come to share tonight with Lila and me." I reached for her hand and motioned for her to rise from her chair so she was standing in front of me. Very slowly, taking a few deep breaths, I reached into my suit pocket and pulled out a small black box. Locking my gaze with the woman who had saved me from a lifetime of darkness, I lowered to one knee, never taking my eyes from her. Hers widened in disbelief at first, and then a lone tear escaped and trickled down her cheek.

"Lila, I resigned myself to the life I was forced into when I was just a young man. I shut down and cut everyone from my life out of total and utter fear. I thought I was destined to live in the shadows until I took my last breath. But you've shone your light into my world, chasing all my demons away." She was full-on crying, and as much as I wanted to get it over with and hold her in my arms, I had to finish. "You will never know how happy you've made me. But if you promise yourself to me, I'll spend every waking moment trying to make you just as happy." Clutching her hand tighter, I moved in closer and asked her what I had been dying to ask for quite some time. "Lila Marie Stone, will you do me the greatest honor of becoming my wife?"

There was silence.

For some of the longest seconds of my life.

My hands started to sweat the longer she didn't speak.

"No." Her tears continued to fall. My breath caught in my throat and I swear my heart stopped beating. I didn't dare look anywhere but up into her lovely face for fear I'd lose my shit right in front of everyone. My hands started to tremble and my vision became a little cloudy, but still, I kept my eyes locked on her, our connection never broken.

After what seemed like forever, when she'd finally composed herself, she parted her lips. "You're the one who will be doing *me* the greatest honor of becoming my husband. You are the other half of me, and I couldn't imagine my life without you in it for the rest of my days on this earth."

Jesus fucking Christ! This woman is going to be the death of me. I wasn't going to lie; my eyes filled up quickly when I thought she refused my proposal. Thankfully, I had enough strength to keep the tears at bay, not wanting anyone to witness the emotional barrage that almost made an appearance.

I removed the five-carat ring from the box and put it on her left hand. She almost hyperventilated when she took a closer look, smiling at me as I rose from my knee. I leaned in and captured her mouth. As soon as our lips met, I heard everyone's excitement behind us. They were shouting "Congratulations," their applause almost drowning out their words. Tilting Lila's face upward toward mine once we broke apart, I saw she was battling with a deep sadness. I knew she was happy about what had just happened, so I was confused. "What's wrong, honey?" I intently perused her face.

"It's . . . I . . . I wish my mom was here with me. I know she'd be so happy for me. For us." She leaned into me and snuggled her head on my chest. "This would be the story of all stories, because it finally came true." I hugged her close, trying to provide the safe, loving escape she so desperately needed.

We all celebrated our new engagement well into the evening. I was anxious to get her home, though. All her attention was stolen from me with Eve and Beverly asking her all sorts of wedding questions. Ellie and Gabriella bonded quickly, both laughing at Lila's overwhelmed expression.

At one point, I was leaning against the bar, waiting for another round of drinks. Watching Lila and the others laugh and tell stories, I was jolted from the scene when a familiar voice sounded to my left.

"Maxwell? Is that you, man?" a gruff voice asked. Turning my head, my eyes landed on one of my oldest and dearest friends, Lucas Hullen. I hadn't seen him in almost ten years. He looked the same, only a few years added to the distinguished guy he always was. His jet-black hair was a bit longer, brushing just over his collar.

Seeing him there instantly took me back to the good ol' days. When everything was simple. No worries except passing our exams and figuring out where we were going to go on spring break.

Shit! Time really does fly by. Although, in my case, I wasn't having any fun—not for the past eight years, anyway. I wouldn't change a thing, however, because my life's path brought me to Lila.

Turning all my attention on Lucas, I swung around and shook his hand, pulling him in for a big hug. "How are you?" I asked as we continued to stare at one another. I really missed his friendship over the years, although it was by necessity I'd cut ties with him.

"Holy shit! I can't believe my eyes. Mason Maxwell is actually standing in front of me." He laughed and punched me on the arm. "So, you're not really dead."

"People said I was dead?"

"Yeah, we all thought you bit the big one. Although we were never sure how it happened."

"I would've gone with a tragic folding chair accident," I joked.

It was good to see him, and I wasn't going to let another second go by without securing plans for us to catch up. "Do you live around here still?"

"Yeah, about a half hour away. By the way, what are you doing here? Are you with someone?" He scanned the room, landing on exactly the group of women who were there with me.

"Actually, I'm here with my fiancée and some friends." *Wow!* It was going to take me some time to get used to saying *fiancée*, but I loved the sound of it.

"Well, congratulations. When did it happen?"

I looked down at my watch, and said, "About four hours ago." Laughing again and engaged in idle chitchat, I hadn't even noticed when Lila walked up behind me until she cleared her throat to get my attention. I turned and pulled her in close, my arm wrapped possessively around her waist. If I remembered anything about Lucas, it was he was a big playboy. His rugged good looks attracted every woman's attention. I was simply claiming Lila in front of him, just to be safe.

"Hi, babe. How are you feeling?"

"I'm a little tired." She looked quickly between Lucas and me, before asking, "I don't want to interrupt your conversation or anything, but do you think we could head home soon?" I saw her eyes keep flitting back toward Lucas, and it was making me a little uneasy, annoyed even. She was mine, so why was she eye-balling him? Before I became even more agitated, she placed her hand on my chest, leaned in, and gave me a big kiss. She knew me well enough to know what to do to calm me right down. "Who is your friend?"

I didn't get a word out before he introduced himself, extending his hand to her. "Hi, I'm Lucas Hullen. I'm an old buddy of Mason's."

In my opinion, he held her hand a little too long, and when I physically separated them, he laughed. He enjoyed riling me up.

As I was about to say something in jest, warning him she was all mine, we were interrupted by Ellie walking up next to Lila, her eyes solely focused on Lucas. I knew that look, had seen it too many times to count. She wanted a piece of him, and knowing my buddy, it was as good as a done deal.

"Mason," she cooed. "Who is your friend?" Her eyes swept over him, her thoughts on display for anyone to see. The intensity between both of them was instant, and it made me uncomfortable. Glancing at Lila, she appeared amused, knowing full well what her aunt's intentions were.

"Lucas, this is Ellie. Ellie . . . Lucas." As with Lila, he shook her hand, but he pulled her in close and kissed her cheek.

"Pleasure to meet you, Ellie. Are you Lila's sister?" he asked.

She looked flattered, of course, even though she knew she could definitely pass as Lila's sibling, only being ten years her senior. "Aren't you a charmer?" She explained she was her aunt.

They were not subtle with their flirtations. Not at all. Before I could excuse myself, Lucas leaned in and whispered something in her ear, causing her breath to quicken.

Okay, we're outta here. I told him to give me a call and we'd set something up very soon. Pulling my fiancée away, I nuzzled her ear, and whispered what I was going to do to her once I got her home.

It was another twenty minutes before we said all our goodbyes, thanking everyone again for sharing the night with us. As I glanced around the restaurant, I noticed Ellie still engaged in conversation with Lucas. God only knew what they were talking about.

Lucas and I were thick as thieves years before, and I knew certain things about him, things that were kept within our circle of friends. Well, and with the women he'd chosen to share them with. He had a taste for the darker excitements, certain proclivities that were not for the faint of heart, but I never judged him. As long as everyone involved was consensual, have at it. But it was a little different when it was someone who was going to soon be part of my family.

I felt I owed it to Lila to protect Ellie. I found my opportunity when Lucas excused himself to visit the men's room. Letting go of Lila's hand, I kissed her on the cheek and told her I would be right back. Glancing after me, her curiosity getting the best of her, she relaxed when she realized I was going to see her aunt.

"Ellie," I started. "Listen, I want to tell you something about Lucas." Her brow furrowed for a split second before a wide smile broke out across her face. "What's so funny?" I asked as I started doing some fidgeting of my own.

"If you're going to warn me about his *preferences*, don't worry. He told me."

"He told you?" I practically shouted. Lowering my voice immediately before anyone caught on, I moved in closer. "*What* did he tell you?"

She gripped my shoulder and leaned in. "He told me what he told me. Don't worry about me, Mason. Really. I appreciate it, but I'm a big girl." As I was about to push further, Lucas came around the corner, his sights set on the two of us. I quickly saw something glint in his eyes, but I couldn't put my finger on what it was.

"Lucas, I need a word," I said, but Ellie stepped in front of me, pretty much telling me to back off. When I didn't step away, she called for her niece.

Nice—way to play that card.

Lila's hurried steps took me off-guard and I stepped back, almost tripping over my own goddamn feet.

"What's the matter, Aunt Ellie?" she asked, her gaze flitting from Lucas, to her aunt, to me. She opened her pretty little mouth to say something else, when Ellie cut in.

"Can you please remove your concerned, loving, but very

overbearing fiancé?" Her jest instantly calmed Lila, making her smile as she continued to stare at all three of us. Reaching over, she linked her fingers with mine and tugged me away. I went . . . reluctantly. Locking eyes with Lucas, I was trying to give him a warning look, but the only thing that fucker did was wink at me as he wrapped his arm around Ellie's waist and pulled her in close, kissing her temple.

She laughed. Would she still be amused when he exposed all of himself to her? There was nothing I could do. I tried, but in reality, everyone involved was a grown-ass adult.

Shaking my head and focusing on my lovely fiancée, we made our way back toward the table. Everyone was getting ready to leave, and we were fortunate enough to walk out with them.

Hugging and kissing goodbye, we promised to have everyone over to the house for dinner in the next week. My sister chose to stay in a hotel, even though I pleaded with her to stay with us. She joked she'd be more comfy staying in a place where they delivered food to her, whenever she wanted. I think the real reason she didn't stay at the house was because she didn't want to overwhelm Lila, a fact I had to be grateful for at least.

On the drive home, all I kept thinking was how I was the luckiest son of a bitch in the entire world. The fact the glorious creature sitting next to me had not only put up with my shit since she'd met me, but decided to actually give me her heart, was simply amazing.

Glancing over, I could tell she was wiped, even though she was doing her best to keep her eyes open. I tried to get us home as quick as possible. My thoughts instantly flew to her lying across our bed, naked and waiting for me to bury myself inside her. My cock twitched in my pants, and as soon as I palmed myself, trying not to let the beast get too wild, I heard her laugh.

"Is someone getting excited?"

"Always."

The sudden gleam in her eyes had me breaking every traffic rule, desperate to feel her against me, over and over again.

AS WE LAY there, so wrapped up in each other I couldn't tell where she ended and I began, my heart slowed to a steady pace. I had taken her three times before I decided to let her get some rest. She told me I was simply insatiable, kissing me sweetly before rolling over on her side, giving me yet another glorious look at that body of hers.

I kissed her shoulder. "I love you, baby. Now and forever."

"Love you, too." Her words barely escaped her lips before sleep took her under. I was too excited about our future to fall asleep right away. Lying on my back with my hands nestled behind my head, I stared off into the dark space, dreaming of a life I always thought was impossible.

I'd resigned myself to a life of loneliness and misery. There were a few times I thought about checking out, thinking it would be better than dealing with the shitty circumstances I was forced into. The women's cries were enough to haunt me in my dreams, but even in reality, I was always aware . . . aware I was no better than the man who had forced me into that world. Or at least that was how I thought before Lila came into my life.

She was the one my soul was searching for the whole time.

She was my connection to another life, one filled with endless love and happiness.

She was my salvation.

She was my unwavering redemption.

EPILOGUE

FOUR MONTHS PASSED since the night I asked Lila to be my wife. Four months of bliss. Four months of us getting to know each other's quirks, learning how the other dealt with stressful situations. I liked to claim her, ravaging her entire body when the world got to be too much for me. She, on the other hand, liked to drink a glass of wine and binge on my peanut butter brittle ice cream. Then she'd attack me, seeking out her release underneath me, or on top of me. Whatever she was in the mood for.

All I wanted to do was whisk her away to some foreign land for months on end, but our daily lives required our attention. I was kept busy with my everyday business dealings, sometimes finding time to help Lila with the charity. If possible, she was even busier, working countless long hours making sure everything was running smoothly, that all the necessary resources were available to the people who needed them. But I'd never seen her happier. She wanted to do it for the victims who'd been saved, but also as a tribute to those who were lost to that world. She felt by saving just one woman's life, no one's death was in vain.

The one room in the house I'd kept locked up tight was converted into an office for her. A space that harbored the worst part of me now shone bright with the good we were doing for others. I'd sent everything I had in boxes to the police, giving them more than enough information to help take down the whole dark organization. I made sure to keep it anonymous, because I didn't want any more ties to that past.

"Honey, what do you want to eat tonight?" Since she'd been living here, we'd made a few adjustments. We decided to give Norma an additional two days off during the week, continuing to pay her the same amount. Lila didn't want to impact her finances simply because she wanted a little more privacy for the two of us. I told her I didn't cook and unless she wanted to take over for Norma, we were going to be eating a lot of takeout. She was used to cooking for her mom, so she said it was no big deal; she wanted to do it.

"I'm good with whatever you're in the mood for, babe." I came around the corner and strolled into the kitchen. Her hair was pulled up in a messy bun, and she wore pink lounge pants and a white T-shirt, no bra. Bent over, she scoured the refrigerator looking for the night's meal.

God, she was fucking sexy.

Walking up behind her, I grabbed her waist and pulled her into me, growling in her ear while I pushed myself into her ass. "What do you think you're doing, Mr. Maxwell?" She reached back and tangled her hands into the thick of my hair, giving a slight tug to tell me she was on board with what I was thinking.

"I know what I want for dinner."

"You do?" She pushed her ass farther against my cock.

"Yes." I turned her around and crashed my mouth to hers, nibbling on her lip until she gave me entrance into her sweet warmth.

She broke free for some much-needed air. "And what, pray tell, is that?"

I lifted her on top of the island, spread her legs, and stepped in between. I was instantly taken back to the night I'd basically accosted her in that very kitchen, while she teased me with *my* ice cream. I wanted her so bad that night. But we weren't ready to be together, too much baggage weighing me down. Thankfully, she didn't give up on me. I didn't know what I would've done if she disappeared from my life altogether.

Not wanting to think about it anymore, I answered her sultry question. "I want you for dinner . . . and dessert. I want to taste you everywhere. I want your need to coat my tongue." I moved closer and claimed her mouth again, my fingers pinching her pebbled nipples. "I need you so bad," I whispered against her swollen lips.

"Then take me."

And I did, over and over again, each time thanking God above she was so forcefully shoved into my life.

THE END

NOTE TO READER

IF YOU ARE a new reader of my work, thank you so much for taking a chance on me. If I'm old news to you, thank you for continuing to support me. It truly means everything.

If you've enjoyed this book, or any of my other stories, please consider leaving a review. It doesn't have to be long at all. A sentence or two will do just fine. Of course, if you wish to elaborate, feel free to write as much as you want. ☺

If you would like to be notified of my upcoming releases, cover reveals, giveaways, etc, be sure to sign up for my newsletter: https://www.subscribepage.com/snelsonnewsletter

ACKNOWLEDGEMENTS

FIRST OFF, I would like to thank my husband for being patient with me this whole time. I released one book after another, spending countless hours locked away in my office. Thanks for holding your tongue when I know you wanted nothing more than to yell for me to join the land of the living. I love you!

A huge thank you to my family and friends for always being there when I wanted to talk about the book. Your love and support mean the world to me. I don't know what I would do without you!

Kayla, thank you so much for your comments and suggestions. You definitely helped me polish Mason and Lila's story. You're simply amazing!

Clarise (CT Cover Creations), we've come a long way together and I continuously look forward to our next project together. This cover is gorgeous!

Kiki, and all of the amazing ladies at The Next Step PR- I don't even want to think about navigating this wonderful book world without your encouragement, knowledge and support.

Ruth, I'm one lucky woman to have you in my corner. You help me more than you know and I'd be lost without you. I look forward to our chats and love that you love my men as much as I do. ☺

To all of the bloggers who have shared my work, I'm forever indebted to you. You ladies are simply wonderful!

To all of you who have reached out to me to let me know how much you loved my stories, I am beyond humbled. Thank you so much, and I'll continue to do my best to bring you stories you can lose yourself in, even if it's only for a few hours.

And last but not least, I would like to thank you, the reader. If this is the first book you've read from me, I hope you enjoy it. If this is yet another story from me you've taken a chance on . . . THANK YOU from the bottom of my heart!

ABOUT THE AUTHOR

S. NELSON GREW up with a love of reading and a very active imagination, never putting pen to paper, or fingers to keyboard until 2013.

Her passion to create was overwhelming, and within a few months she'd written her first novel, Stolen Fate. When she isn't engrossed in creating one of the many stories rattling around inside her head, she loves to read and travel as much as she can. She lives in the Northeast with her husband and two dogs, enjoying the ever changing seasons.

If you would like to follow or contact her please feel free to do so at the following:

Website:
www.snelsonauthor.com

Email Address:
snelsonauthor8@gmail.com

Also on Facebook, Goodreads, Amazon, Instagram and Twitter

S. Nelson

Made in the USA
Middletown, DE
26 April 2022